W9-ADE-326

A Confederate General from Big Sur

A Confederate General from Big Sur

by

Richard Brautigan

GROVE PRESS, INC.   NEW YORK

Copyright © 1964 by Richard Brautigan

All Rights Reserved

Library of Congress Catalog Card Number : 64–24078

Acknowledgment is made to Ezra J. Warner and the
Louisiana State University Press for permission
to reprint the tables on pages 11 and 12 and
the biographies of Samuel Bell Maxey and
General Hugh Weedon Mercer on pages 29 and 30
from *Generals in Gray*.
Three chapters from this book were
first published in *Tri-Quarterly*.

NO part of this book may be reproduced, for any reason,
by any means, including any method of photographic
reproduction, without the permission of the publisher.

First Evergreen Edition 1968

Twelfth Printing

Manufactured in the United States of America

DISTRIBUTED BY RANDOM HOUSE, INC., NEW YORK

to my daughter
Ianthe

CONTENTS

Prologue

Attrition's Old Sweet Song

"THE RECORDS EXHIBIT that 425 individuals received appointment by the President to one of the four grades of general, of whom 299 were in grade at the end of the war. The attrition is accounted for as follows:

Killed in action or died of wounds	77
Resigned	19
Died by accident or from natural causes	15
Appointments cancelled	5
Declined appointment	3
Killed in "personal encounters"	2
Assassinated	1
Committed suicide	1
Dropped	1
Retired by reason of wounds	1
Reverted to rank of colonel	1
Total	**126**"

I Mean, What Do You Do Besides Being a Confederate General?

"Lawyers, jurists 129
Professional soldiers 125
Businessmen (including bankers,
    manufacturers, and merchants) 55
Farmers, planters 42
Politicians 24
Educators 15
Civil engineers 13
Students 6
Doctors 4
Ministers 3
Frontiersmen, peace officers 3
Indian agents 2
Naval officers 2
Editor 1
Soldier of fortune 1
                        ———
                Total 425"

Part One

A Confederate General from Big Sur

A Confederate General from Big Sur

WHEN I FIRST HEARD about Big Sur I didn't know that it was a member of the Confederate States of America. I had always thought that Georgia, Arkansas, Mississippi, Florida, Alabama, Louisiana, South Carolina, Virginia, Tennessee, North Carolina and Texas were the Confederacy, and let it go at that. I had no idea that Big Sur was also a member.

Big Sur the twelfth member of the Confederate States of America? Frankly, it's hard to believe that those lonely stark mountains and clifflike beaches of California were rebels, that the redwood trees and the ticks and the cormorants waved a rebel flag along that narrow hundred miles of land that lies between Monterey and San Luis Obispo.

The Santa Lucia Mountains, that thousand-year-old flophouse for mountain lions and lilacs, a hotbed of Secession? The Pacific Ocean along there, that million-year-old skid row for abalone and kelp, sending representatives back to the Confederate Congress in Richmond, Virginia?

I've heard that the population of Big Sur in those Civil

15

War days was mostly just some Digger Indians. I've heard that the Digger Indians down there didn't wear any clothes. They didn't have any fire or shelter or culture. They didn't grow anything. They didn't hunt and they didn't fish. They didn't bury their dead or give birth to their children. They lived on roots and limpets and sat pleasantly out in the rain.

I can imagine the expression on General Robert E. Lee's face when this gang showed up, bearing strange gifts from the Pacific Ocean.

It was during the second day of the Battle of the Wilderness. A. P. Hill's brave but exhausted Confederate troops had been hit at daybreak by Union General Hancock's II Corps of 30,000 men. A. P. Hill's troops were shattered by the attack and fell back in defeat and confusion along the Orange Plank Road.

Twenty-eight-year-old Colonel William Poague, the South's fine artillery man, waited with sixteen guns in one of the few clearings in the Wilderness, Widow Tapp's farm. Colonel Poague had his guns loaded with antipersonnel ammunition and opened fire as soon as A. P. Hill's men had barely fled the Orange Plank Road.

The Union assault funneled itself right into a vision of sculptured artillery fire, and the Union troops suddenly found pieces of flying marble breaking their centers and breaking their edges. At the instant of contact, history transformed their bodies into statues. They didn't like it, and the assault began to back up along the Orange Plank Road. What a nice name for a road.

Colonel Poague and his men held their ground alone without any infantry support, and no way out, caring not for the name of the road. They were there forever and General Lee was right behind them in the drifting marble dust of their guns. He was waiting for General Longstreet's arrival with reinforcements. Longstreet's men were hours late.

Then the first of them arrived. Hood's old Texas Brigade led by John Gregg came on through the shattered forces of A. P. Hill, and these Texans were surprised because A. P. Hill's men were shock troops of the Confederate Army, and here they were in full rout.

"What troops are you, my boys?" Lee said.

"The Texans!" the men yelled and quickly formed into battle lines. There were less than a thousand of them and they started forward toward that abyss of Federal troops.

Lee was in motion with them, riding his beautiful gray horse, Traveller, a part of the wave. But they stopped him and shouted, "Lee to the rear! Lee to the rear!"

They turned him around and sent him back to spend the last years of his life quietly as the president of Washington College, later to be called Washington and Lee.

Then they went forward possessed only by animal fury, without any regard now for their human shadows. It was a little late for things like that.

The Texans suffered 50 per cent casualties in less than ten minutes, but they contained the Union. It was like putting your finger in the ocean and having it stop, but only briefly because Appomattox Courthouse waited less than a year away, resting now in its gentle anonymity.

When Lee got to the rear of the lines, there were the 8th Big Sur Volunteer Heavy Root Eaters reporting for duty. The air around them was filled with the smell of roots and limpets. The 8th Big Sur Volunteer Heavy Root Eaters reported like autumn to the Army of Northern Virginia.

They all gathered around Lee's horse and stared in amazement, for it was the first time that they had ever seen a horse. One of the Digger Indians offered Traveller a limpet to eat.

When I first heard about Big Sur I didn't know that it was part of the defunct Confederate States of America, a country that went out of style like an idea or a lampshade or some kind of food that people don't cook any more, once the favorite dish in thousands of homes.

It was only through a Lee-of-another-color, Lee Mellon, that I found out the truth about Big Sur. Lee Mellon who is the battle flags and the drums of this book. Lee Mellon: a Confederate general in ruins.

The Tide Teeth of Lee Mellon

IT IS IMPORTANT before I go any further in this military narrative to talk about the teeth of Lee Mellon. They need talking about. During these five years that I have known Lee Mellon, he has probably had 175 teeth in his mouth.

This is due to a truly gifted faculty for getting his teeth knocked out. It almost approaches genius. They say that John Stuart Mill could read Greek when he was three years old and had written a history of Rome at the age of six and a half.

But the amazing thing about Lee Mellon's teeth is their strange and constantly moving placement in the many and varied dentures those poor teeth briefly get to call home. I would meet him one day on Market Street and he would have just one upper left tooth in his face, and then I'd see him again, months later on Grant Avenue, and he'd have three lower right teeth and one upper right tooth.

I'd see him again just back from Big Sur, and he'd have four upper front teeth, and two lower left teeth, and then after a few weeks in San Francisco, he'd be wearing the upper plate without any teeth in it at all, wearing the plate just so he would have a head start on gristle, and so that his cheeks wouldn't collapse in on his mouth.

I've adjusted to this teeth fantasia always happening to him, and so now everytime I see him, I have a good look at his mouth to see how things are going with him, to see if he has been working, what books he has been reading, whether Sara Teasdale or *Mein Kampf,* and whom he has been sleeping with: blondes or brunettes.

Lee Mellon told me that once in Modern Times, he'd had all his teeth in his mouth at the same time for a whole day. He was driving a tractor in Kansas, back and forth across a field of wheat, and his brand-new lower plate felt a little funny in his mouth, so he took it out and put it into his shirt pocket. The teeth fell out of his pocket, and he backed the tractor over them.

Lee Mellon told me rather sadly that after he had discovered that the teeth were gone from his shirt pocket, it took him almost an hour to find them, and when he found them, they weren't worth finding at all.

The First Time I Met Lee Mellon

I MET LEE MELLON five years ago in San Francisco. It was spring. He had just "hitch-hiked" up from Big Sur. Along the way a rich queer stopped and picked Lee Mellon up in a sports car. The rich queer offered Lee Mellon ten dollars to commit an act of oral outrage.

Lee Mellon said all right and they stopped at some lonely place where there were trees leading back into the mountains, joining up with a forest way back in there, and then the forest went over the top of the mountains.

"After you," Lee Mellon said, and they walked back into the trees, the rich queer leading the way. Lee Mellon picked up a rock and bashed the rich queer in the head with it.

"Ouch!" the rich queer said and fell on the ground. That hurt, and the rich queer began begging for his life.

"Spare me! Spare me! I'm just a lonely little rich queer who wanted to have some fun. I never hurt anyone."

"Stop blubbering," Lee Mellon said. "And give me all

your money and the keys to your car. That's all I want anyway, you rich queer."

The rich queer gave Lee Mellon $235.00 and the keys to his car and his watch.

Lee Mellon hadn't said anything about the rich queer's watch, but figuring that his birthday was coming up soon, he'd be twenty-three, Lee Mellon took the watch and put it in his pocket.

The rich queer was having the greatest time of his life. A tall, young, good-looking, dashing, toothless raider was taking all his money and his car and his watch away.

It would make a wonderful story to tell his other rich queer friends. He could show the bump on his head and point to the place where his watch had been.

The rich queer reached up and felt the bump on his head. It was rising like a biscuit. The rich queer hoped the bump wouldn't go away for a long time.

"I'm going now," Lee Mellon said. "And you sit right where you are until tomorrow morning. If you move an inch, I'll come back here and run over you a couple of times with my car. I'm a desperate man, and I like nothing better in this world than to run over rich queers."

"I won't move until tomorrow morning," the rich queer said. This made sense to him. After all Lee Mellon did appear to be quite a mean man, for all his good looks.

"I won't move an inch," the rich queer promised.

"That's a good rich queer," Lee Mellon said and abandoned the car in Monterey and took a bus on into San Francisco.

When I met the young raider for the first time, he had been on a four-day drunk with his confiscated funds. He bought a bottle of whiskey and we went into an alley to drink it. Things are done like that in San Francisco.

Lee Mellon and I yakked up a storm and became close

friends immediately. He said he was looking for a place to live. He still had some of the rich queer's money left.

I said that there was a vacant room for rent under the attic where I lived over on Leavenworth Street, and Lee Mellon said, howdy neighbor.

Lee Mellon knew that there was no danger of the rich queer ever going to the police. "The rich queer's probably still sitting down there at Big Sur," Lee Mellon said. "I hope he doesn't starve to death."

Augustus Mellon, CSA

THE FIRST TIME I MET Lee Mellon the night went away with every totem drop of the whiskey. When dawn came we were down on the Embarcadero and it was raining. Seagulls started it all, that gray screeching, almost like banners, running with the light. There was a ship going someplace. It was a Norwegian ship.

Perhaps it was going back to Norway, carrying the hides of 163 cable cars, as part of the world commerce deal. Ah, trade: one country exchanging goods with another country, just like in grade school. They traded a rainy spring morning in Oslo for 163 cable car hides from San Francisco.

Lee Mellon looked at the sky. Sometimes when you meet people for the first time, they stare at the sky. He stared for a long time. "What?" I said, because I wanted to be his friend.

"Just seagulls," he said. "That one," and pointed at a seagull, but I couldn't tell which one it was for there were

24

many, summoning their voices to the dawn. Then he said nothing for a while.

Yes, one could think of seagulls. We were awfully tired, hung over and still drunk. One could think of seagulls. It's really a very simple thing to do . . . seagulls: past, present and future passing almost like drums to the sky.

We stopped at a little cafe and got some coffee. The coffee was brought to us by the world's ugliest waitress. I gave her an imaginary name: Thelma. I do things like that.

My name is Jesse. Any attempt to describe her would be against my better judgment, but in her own way she seemed to belong in that cafe with steam rising like light out of our coffee.

Helen of Troy would have looked out of place. "What's Helen of Troy doing in here?" some longshoreman would have asked. He wouldn't have understood. So Thelma it was for the likes of us.

Lee Mellon told me that he was born in Meridian, Mississippi, and grew up in Florida, Virginia and North Carolina. "Near Asheville," he said. "That's Thomas Wolfe country."

"Yeah," I said.

Lee Mellon didn't have any Southern accent. "You don't have much of a Southern accent," I said.

"That's right, Jesse. I read a lot of Nietzsche, Schopenhauer and Kant when I was a kid," Lee Mellon said.

I guess in some strange way that was supposed to get rid of a Southern accent. Lee Mellon thought so, anyway. I couldn't argue because I had never tried a Southern accent against the German philosophers.

"When I was sixteen years old I stole into classes at the University of Chicago and lived with two highly cultured young Negro ladies who were freshmen," Lee Mellon said.

"We all slept in the same bed together. It helped me get rid of my Southern accent."

"Sounds like it might do the trick," I said, not knowing exactly what I was saying.

Thelma, the world's ugliest waitress, came over and asked us if we wanted some breakfast. The hotcakes were good and the bacon and eggs were good and would fill you up. "Hit the spot," Thelma said.

I had the hotcakes and Lee Mellon had the hotcakes and the bacon and eggs and some more hotcakes. He did not pay any attention to Thelma and continued to talk about the South.

He told me that he had lived on a farm near Spotsylvania, Virginia, and had spent a lot of time as a child going over the places where the Battle of the Wilderness had been fought.

"My great grandfather fought there," he said. "He was a general. A Confederate general and a damn good one, too. I was raised on stories of General Augustus Mellon, CSA. He died in 1910. The same year Mark Twain died. That was the year of Halley's Comet. He was a general. Have you ever heard of General Augustus Mellon?"

"No, but that's really something," I said. "A Confederate general . . . gee."

"Yeah, we Mellons have always been very proud of General Augustus Mellon. There's a statue of him some place, but we don't know where it is.

"My Uncle Benjamin spent two years trying to find the statue. He traveled all over the South in an old truck and slept in the back. That statue is probably in some park covered with vines. They don't pay enough respect to our honored dead. Our great heroes."

Our plates were empty now like orders for a battle not yet conceived, in a war not yet invented. I said farewell to the world's ugliest waitress, but Lee Mellon insisted on paying the check. He took a good look at Thelma.

Perhaps he was seeing her for the first time, and as I remember, he hadn't said anything about her while she was bringing the coffee and breakfast to us.

"I'll give you a dollar for a kiss," Lee Mellon said while she was giving him the change for ten dollars of the rich queer's rock-on-the-head money.

"Sure," she said, without smiling or being embarrassed or acting out of the way or anything. It was just as if the Dollar Lee Mellon Kissing Business were an integral part of her job.

Lee Mellon gave her a great big kiss. Neither one of them cracked, opened or celebrated a smile. He did not show in any manner that he was joking. I went along with him. The subject was never brought up by either one of us, so it *almost* stays there.

As we walked along the Embarcadero the sun came out like memory and began to recall the rain back to the sky and Lee Mellon said, "I know where we can get four pounds of muscatel for one dollar and fifteen cents."

We went there. It was an old Italian wineshop on Powell Street, just barely open. There was a row of wine barrels against the wall. The center of the shop led back into darkness. I believe the darkness came off the wine barrels smelling of Chianti, zinfandel and Burgundy.

"A half gallon of muscatel," Lee Mellon said.

The old man who ran the shop got the wine off a shelf behind him. He wiped some imaginary dust off the bottle. Like a strange plumber he was used to selling wine.

We left with the muscatel and went up to the Ina Coolbrith Park on Vallejo Street. She was a poet contemporary of Mark Twain and Brett Harte during that great San Francisco literary renaissance of the 1860s.

Then Ina Coolbrith was an Oakland librarian for thirty-two years and first delivered books into the hands of the child Jack London. She was born in 1841 and died in 1928: "Loved Laurel-Crowned Poet of California," and she was the same woman whose husband took a shot at her with a rifle in 1861. He missed.

"Here's to General Augustus Mellon, Flower of Southern Chivalry and Lion of the Battlefield!" Lee Mellon said, taking the cap off four pounds of muscatel.

We drank the four pounds of muscatel in the Ina Coolbrith Park, looking down Vallejo Street to San Francisco Bay and how the sunny morning was upon it and a barge of railroad cars going across to Marin County.

"What a warrior," Lee Mellon said, putting the last ⅓ ounce of muscatel, "the corner," in his mouth.

Having a slight interest in the Civil War and motivated by my new companion, I said, "I know a book that has all the Confederate generals in it. All 425 of them," I said. "It's down at the library. Let's go down and see what General Augustus Mellon pulled off in the war."

"Great idea, Jesse," Lee Mellon said. "He was my great grandfather. I want to know all about him. He was a Lion of the Battlefield. General Augustus Mellon! Hurray for the heroic deeds he performed in the War between the States! Hurray! Hurray! Hurray! HURRAY!"

Figure two pounds of muscatel apiece at twenty per cent alcohol: forty proof. We were still very rocky from a night of whiskey drinking. That's two pounds of muscatel multipled, squared and envisioned. This can all be worked out with computers.

The librarian looked at us when we came into the library and groped a volume off a shelf: *Generals in Gray* by Ezra J. Warner. The biographies of the 425 generals were in alphabetic order and we turned to where General Augustus

Mellon would be. The librarian was debating whether or not to call the police.

We found General Samuel Bell Maxey on the left flank and his story went something like this: *Samuel Bell Maxey was born at Tompkinsville, Kentucky, March 30, 1825. He was graduated from West Point in the class of 1846, and was brevetted for gallantry in the war with Mexico. In 1849 he resigned his commission to study law. In 1857 he and his father, who was also an attorney, moved to Texas, where they practiced in partnership until the outbreak of the Civil War. Resigning a seat in the Texas senate, the younger Maxey organized the 9th Texas Infantry, and with rank of colonel joined the forces of General Albert Sidney Johnston in Kentucky. He was promoted brigadier general to rank from March 4, 1862. He served in East Tennessee, at Port Hudson, and in the Vicksburg campaign, under General J. E. Johnston. In December 1863 Maxey was placed in command of Indian Territory, and for his effective reorganization of the troops there, with which he participated in the Red River campaign, he was assigned to duty as a major general by General Kirby Smith on April 18, 1864. He was not, however, subsequently appointed to that rank by the President. After the war General Maxey resumed the practice of law in Paris, Texas, and in 1873 declined appointment to the state bench. Two years later he was elected to the United States Senate, where he served two terms, being defeated for re-election in 1887. He died at Eureka Springs, Arkansas, August 16, 1895, and is buried in Paris, Texas.*

And on the right flank we found General Hugh Weedon Mercer and his story went something like this: *Hugh Weedon Mercer, a grandson of the Revolutionary General Hugh Mercer, was born at "The Sentry Box," Fredericksburg, Virginia, on November 27, 1808. He was graduated third in the class of 1828 at West Point, and was stationed*

*for some time in Savannah, Georgia, where he married into
a local family. He resigned his commission on April 30, 1835
and settled in Savannah. From 1841 until the outbreak of
the Civil War he was cashier of the Planters' Bank there.
Upon the secession of Georgia, Mercer entered Confederate
service as colonel of the 1st Georgia Volunteers. He was
promoted brigadier general on October 29, 1861. During the
greater part of the war, with a brigade of three Georgia
regiments, General Mercer commanded at Savannah, but he
and his brigade took part in the Atlanta campaign of 1864,
first in W. H. T. Walker's division and then in Cleburne's.
On account of poor health he accompanied General Hardee
to Savannah after the battle of Jonesboro, and saw no
further field duty. Paroled at Macon, Georgia, May 13,
1865, General Mercer returned to banking in Savannah the
following year. He moved to Baltimore in 1869, where he
spent three years as a commission merchant. His health
further declined, and he spent the last five years of his life
in Baden-Baden, Germany. He died there on June 9, 1877.
His remains were returned to Savannah for burial in Bona-
venture Cemetery.*

But in the center of the line there was no General
Augustus Mellon. There had obviously been a retreat during
the night. Lee Mellon was crushed. The librarian was staring
intently at us. Her eyes seemed to have grown a pair of
glasses.

"It can't be," Lee Mellon said. "It just can't be."

"Maybe he was a colonel," I said. "There were a lot of
Southern colonels. Being a colonel was a good thing. You
know, Southern colonels and all. Colonel Something Fried
Chicken." I was trying to make it easier for him. It's quite
a thing to lose a Confederate general and gain a colonel
instead.

Perhaps even a major or a lieutenant. Of course I didn't

say anything about the major or lieutenant business to him. That probably would have made him start crying. The librarian was looking at us.

"He fought in the Battle of the Wilderness. He was just great," Lee Mellon said. "He cut the head off a Yankee captain with one whack."

"That's quite something," I said. "They probably just overlooked him. A mistake was made. Some records were burned or something happened. There was a lot of confusion. That's probably it."

"You bet," Lee Mellon said. "I know there was a Confederate general in my family. There had to be a Mellon general fighting for his country . . . the beloved South."

"You bet," I said.

The librarian was beginning to pick up the telephone.

"Let's go," I said.

"OK," Lee Mellon said. "You believe there was a Confederate general in my family? Promise me you do. There was a Confederate general in my family!"

"I promise," I said.

I could read the lips of the librarian. She was saying Hello, police? Vaudeville, it was.

We stepped outside rather hurriedly and down the street to anonymous sanctuary among the buildings of San Francisco.

"Promise me till your dying day, you'll believe that a Mellon was a Confederate general. It's the truth. That God-damn book lies! There was a Confederate general in my family!"

"I promise," I said and it was a promise that I kept.

Headquarters

1

THE OLD HOUSE where I took Lee Mellon to live, provided, in its own strange way, lodging befitting a Confederate general from Big Sur, a general who had just successfully fought a small skirmish in the trees above the Pacific Ocean.

The house was owned by a very nice Chinese dentist, but it rained in the front hall. The rain came down through a broken skylight, flooding the hall and warping the hardwood floor.

Whenever the dentist visited the place, he put a pair of blue bib overalls on over his business suit. He kept the overalls in what he called his "tool room," but there weren't any tools there, only the blue overalls hanging on a hook.

He put the overalls on just to collect the rent. They were his uniform. Perhaps he had been a soldier at one time or another.

We showed him where the rain came from and the long puddle leading splash, splash down the hall to the community kitchen in the rear, but he refused to be moved by it.

"There it is," he said philosophically and went away peacefully to take off his overalls and hang them in his "tool room."

After all it was his building. He had pulled thousands of teeth to get the place. He obviously liked the puddle right where it was, and we could not argue with his cheap rent.

2

Even before Lee Mellon made the old place his official San Francisco headquarters in the spring of years ago, the building was already occupied by an interesting group of tenants. I lived alone in the attic.

There was a sixty-one-year-old retired music teacher who lived in the room right underneath the attic. He was Spanish and about him like a weathervane whirled the traditions and attitudes of the Old World.

And he was in his own way, the manager. He had appropriated the job like one would find some old clothes lying outside in the rain, and decide that they were the right size and after they had dried out, they would look quite fashionable.

The day after I moved into the attic, he came upstairs and told me that the noise was driving him crazy. He told me to pack my things quickly and go. He told me that he'd had no idea I had such heavy feet when he rented the place to me. He looked down at my feet and said, "They're too heavy. They'll have to go."

I had no idea either when I rented the attic from the old fart. It seems that the attic had been vacant for years. With all those years of peace and quiet, he probably thought that there was a meadow up there with a warm, gentle wind blowing through the wild flowers, and a bird getting hung up above the trees along the creek.

I bribed his hearing with a phonograph record of Mozart, something with horns, and that took care of him. "I love Mozart," he said, instantly reducing my burden of life.

I could feel my feet beginning to weigh less and less as he smiled at the phonograph record. It smiled back. I now weighed a trifle over seventeen pounds and danced like a giant dandelion in his meadow.

The week after Mozart, he left for a vacation in Spain. He said that he was only going to be gone for three months, but my feet must continue their paths of silence. He said he had ways of knowing, even when he wasn't there. It sounded pretty mysterious.

But his vacation turned out to be longer than he had anticipated because he died on his return to New York. He died on the gangplank, just a few feet away from America. He didn't quite make it. His hat did though. It rolled off his head and down the gangplank and landed, plop, on America.

Poor devil. I heard that it was his heart, but the way the Chinese dentist described the business, it could have been his teeth.

* * *

Though his physical appearance was months away, Lee Mellon's San Francisco headquarters were now secure. They took the old man's things away and the room was empty.

3

There were two other rooms on the second floor. One of them was occupied by a Montgomery Street secretary. She left early in the morning and returned late at night. You never saw her on the weekends.

I believe she was a member of a small acting group and spent most of her spare time rehearsing and performing. One might as well believe that as anything else because there was no way of knowing. She had long ingenue legs, so I'll go on believing she was an actress.

We all shared a bathroom on the second floor, but during the months I lived there, she passed.

4

The other room on the second floor was occupied by a man who always said hello in the morning and good evening at night. It was nice of him. One day in February he went down to the community kitchen and roasted a turkey.

He spent hours basting the bird and preparing a grand meal. Many chestnuts and mushrooms were in evidence. After he was finished he took the bird upstairs with him and never used the kitchen again.

Shortly after that, I believe it was Tuesday, he stopped saying hello in the morning and good evening at night.

5

The bottom floor had one room in the front of the
house. Its windows opened on the street and the shades were
always drawn. An old woman lived in that room. She was
eighty-four and lived quite comfortably on a government
pension of thirty-five cents a month.

She looked so old that she reminded me of a comic book
hero of my childhood: The Heap. It was a World War I
German pilot who was shot down and lay wounded for
months in a bog and was slowly changed by mysterious
juices into a $\frac{7}{8}$ plant and $\frac{1}{8}$ human thing.

The Heap walked around like a mound of moldy hay
and performed good deeds, and of course bullets had no
effect on it. The Heap killed the comic book villains by
giving them a great big hug, then instead of riding classically
away into the sunset like a Western, The Heap lumbered off
into the bog. That's the way the old woman looked.

After she paid her rent out of the generous thirty-five-
cent-a-month government pension, there was just enough
money left over for her to buy bread, tea and celery roots,
which were her main sustenance.

One day out of curiosity I looked up celery roots in a
book called *Let's Eat Right to Keep Fit,* by that goddess of
American grub, Adelle Davis, to see how you could keep
alive on them. You can't.

One hundred grams of celery root contains no vitamins
except 2 mg. of Vitamin C. For minerals, it contains 47 mg.
of calcium, 71 mg. of phosphorous and 0.8 mg. of iron. It
would take a lot of celery roots to make a battleship.

One hundred grams of celery root has for its grand

finale, in *Let's Eat Right to Keep Fit,* three grams of protein and the dramatic total of 38 calories.

The old woman had a little hotplate in her room. She did all her "cooking" in there and never used the community kitchen. A hotplate in a little room is the secret flower of millions of old people in this country. There's a poem by Jules Laforgue about the Luxembourg Gardens. The old woman's hotplate was not that poem.

But her father had been a wealthy doctor in the 19th century and had the first franchise in Italy and France for some wondrous American electrical device.

She could not remember what electrical device it was, but her father had been very proud of getting the franchise and watching the crates being unloaded off a ship.

Unfortunately, he lost all his money trying to sell the electrical devices. It seems that nobody else wanted to have the things in their houses. People were afraid of them, thought they would blow up.

She herself had once been a beautiful woman. There was a photograph of her wearing a dress with a decolletage. Her breasts, her long neck and her face were quite lovely.

Then she was a governess and a language instructor in Italian, French, Spanish and German, the border languages, but now, Heap-like senility covered her and there was only an occasional scrap of meat thrown in to break the celery root tyranny of her last days.

She had never married, but I always called her Mrs. I liked her and once gave her a glass of wine. It had been years. She had no friends or relatives left in the world, and drank the wine very slowly.

She said it was good wine, though it wasn't, and talked of her father's vineyard and the wine that came from those grapes until the thousands of unpurchased American electrical devices had withered the vines.

She told me that the vineyard had been on a hill above the sea, and she liked to go there in the late afternoon and walk down the shadowy rows of grapes. It was the Mediterranean Sea.

In her room she had trunks full of things from olden times. She showed me an illustrated book full of hospitals put out by the Italian Red Cross. There was a photograph of Mussolini in the front of the book. It was a little hard to recognize him because he was not hanging upside down from a light post. She told me that he was a great man, but that he had gone too far. "Never do business with the Germans," she said.

Often she wondered aloud what would happen to her things when she would be dead. Some old salt and pepper shakers with people on them. A bolt of faded cloth. There hadn't been time in 84 years to make a dress or some curtains out of the cloth.

They'll put them inside a celery root and then discover a way of making battleships out of celery roots and over the waves her things will travel.

6

The community kitchen was on the bottom floor in the rear of the house. There was a very large room attached by its own entrance to the kitchen. Before the retired music teacher went to Spain, there was a quiet, typical middle-aged woman who lived in the room, but she left the door from her room to the kitchen open all the time. It was as if the community kitchen were her kitchen and what were strangers doing in it. She was always coming and going and staring.

I liked to cook my meager bachelor meals in privacy, but she always watched. I didn't like it. Who wants to have a quiet, typical, middle-aged woman watching you boil a pathetic can of beef and noodle soup for dinner?

After all it was a community kitchen. When she was cooking in there, I thought it was perfectly natural for her to leave the door open, but when I was cooking in there I thought she should have kept the door closed, for after all it was a community kitchen.

While the music teacher was busy dropping dead in New York, the woman moved and three young girls took the room. One of the girls was quite pretty in a blonde athletic sort of way. The other two girls were uglies.

There were all sorts of men flocking around the pretty one, and because she couldn't handle them all, the other girls got a lot of attention.

I have noticed this pattern time and time again. A pretty girl living with an ugly. If you don't make the pretty one, you're aroused enough to take on the ugly. It throws a lot of action into the corner of the uglies.

That room off the kitchen became quite a hive. The girls had come from a small college somewhere in eastern Washington, and at first they allowed their attentions to be taken up by college and post-college types, mostly the clean-cuts.

Then as the girls grew more sophisticated, as they acclimated themselves to the throbbing pulse of a cosmopolitan city, their attentions naturally switched to bus drivers.

It was pretty funny because there were so many bus drivers hanging around, paying court in their uniforms, that the place looked like the car barn.

Sometimes I would have to cook a meal with four or five bus drivers sitting at the kitchen table, watching me fry a hamburger. One of them absentlymindedly clicking his transfer punch.

A Daring Cavalry Attack on PG&E

ONE MORNING AFTER LEE MELLON had been living below me on Leavenworth Street for a couple of weeks, I woke up and looked around me. The meadow was fading rapidly. The grass had turned brown. The creek was almost dry. The flowers were gone. The trees had fallen over on their sides. I hadn't seen a bird or an animal since the old man died. They all just left.

I decided to go down and wake Lee Mellon up. I got out of bed and put my clothes on. I went down to his room and knocked on the door. I thought we might have some coffee or something.

"Come on in," Lee Mellon said.

I opened the door and Lee Mellon was in the sack with a young girl. Their entwined feet were sticking out one end of the bed. Their heads were sticking out the other end. At first I thought they were fucking and then I could see that they weren't. But I hadn't been far behind. The room smelled like Cupid's gym.

41

I was standing there and then I closed the door.

"This is Susan," Lee Mellon said. "That's my buddy."

"Hello," she said.

The room was all yellow because the shades were pulled down and the sun was shining hard outside. There were all sorts of things thrown all over the room: books, clothes and bottles in cleverly planned disorder. They were maps of important battles to come.

I talked to them for a few minutes. We decided to go downstairs to the community kitchen and have some breakfast.

I stepped outside in the hall while they got dressed, and then we went downstairs together. The girl was tucking in her blouse. Lee Mellon hadn't bothered to tie his shoelaces. They flopped like angleworms all the way down the stairs.

The girl cooked breakfast. Funny, to this very day I remember what she cooked: scrambled eggs with scallions and cream cheese. She made some whole wheat toast and a pot of good coffee. She was very young and cheerful. She had a pretty face and body, though she was a little overweight. Buxom is the right term, but that was just baby fat.

She talked enthusiastically about *In Dubious Battle* by John Steinbeck. "Those poor fruit pickers," the girl said. Lee Mellon agreed with her. After breakfast they went upstairs to talk about their future.

I went downtown to see three movies in a Market Street flea palace. It was a bad habit of mine. From time to time I would get the desire to confuse my senses by watching large flat people crawl back and forth across a huge piece of light, like worms in the intestinal track of a tornado.

I would join the sailors who can't get laid, the old people who make those theaters their solariums, the immobile visionaries, and the poor sick people who come there for the outpatient treatment of watching a pair of Lusitanian mammary glands kiss a set of Titanic capped teeth.

I found three pictures that were the right flavors: a monster picturehelphelp, a cowboy picturebangbang and a dime store romance pictureIloveyou, and found a seat next to a man who was staring up at the ceiling.

The girl stayed for three days with Lee Mellon. She was sixteen years old and came from Los Angeles. She was a Jewess and her father was in the appliance business down in Los Angeles, and was known as the Freezer King of Sepulveda Boulevard.

He showed up at the end of the third day. It seems that the girl had run away from home, and when she had used up the last of her money, she called Poppa on the telephone and said that she was living with a man and they needed money and she gave her father the address where he could send the money.

Before the girl's father took her away, he had a little chat with Lee Mellon. He told Lee Mellon that he didn't want any trouble from this business and he made Lee Mellon promise never to see her again. He gave twenty dollars to Lee Mellon who said thanks.

The Freezer King said that he could build a fire under Lee Mellon if he wanted to, but he didn't want any scandal. "Just don't see her any more and everything will be all right."

"Sure," Lee Mellon said. "I can see your point."

"I don't want any trouble, and you don't want any trouble. We'll just leave it right there," her father said.

"Uh-huh," Lee Mellon said.

The Freezer King took his daughter back to Los Angeles. It had been a fine adventure even though her father had slapped her face in the car and called her a *schicksa*.

A little while after that Lee Mellon moved out of his room because he couldn't pay the rent and went over and lay siege to Oakland. It was a rather impoverished siege that went on for months and was marked by only one offensive maneuver, a daring cavalry attack on the Pacific Gas and Electric Company.

Lee Mellon lived in the abandoned house of a friend who was currently Class C Ping-Pong champion of a rustic California insane asylum. The classifications of A, B or C were determined by the number of shock treatments administered to the patients. The gas and electricity had been turned off in 1937 when the friend's mother had been tucked away for keeping chickens in the house.

Lee Mellon of course didn't have any money to get them turned back on again, so he tunneled his way to the main gas line and tapped it. Then he had a way to cook and heat the place, but he never quite got the energy to put the thing under complete control. Consequently, whenever he turned the gas on with a hastily improvised valve, and put a match to the gas, out jumped a six-foot-long blue flame.

He found an old kerosene lantern and that took care of his light. He had a card to the Oakland Public Library and that took care of his entertainment. He was reading the Russians with that certain heavy tone people put in their voices when they say, "I'm reading the Russians."

There wasn't much food because he had little money to buy it with. Lee Mellon didn't want to get a job. Laying siege to Oakland was difficult enough without going to work. So he went hungry most of the time, but he wouldn't give up his PG&E security. He had to scuffle for his chow: panhandling on the streets and going around to the back doors of restaurants, and walking around looking for money in the gutters.

During his extended siege he abstained from drink and

didn't show much interest in women. Once he said to me, "I haven't been laid in five months." He said it in a matter-of-fact way as if he were commenting on the weather.

Do you think it's going to rain?

No, why should it?

Susan arrived one morning over at Leavenworth Street and said, "I've got to see Lee Mellon. It's very important."

I could see that it was very important. She showed how important it was. The months had gathered at her waist.

"I don't know where he's living," I lied. "He just left one day without leaving a forwarding address," I lied. "I wonder where Lee Mellon is?" I lied.

"Have you seen him around town any?"

"No," I lied. "He's just vanished," I lied.

I couldn't tell her that he was living in Oakland in terrible poverty. His only comfort being that he had tunneled his way to the main gas line and was now enjoying the rather dubious fruit of his labor: a six-foot-long blue flame. And that his eyebrows were gone.

"He's just vanished," I lied. "Everybody wonders where he went," I lied.

"Well, if you see him any place, you tell him I've got to see him. It's very important. I'm staying at the San Geronimo Hotel on Columbus Avenue, Room 34."

She wrote it all down on a piece of paper and gave it to me. I put it in my pocket. She watched me put it in my pocket. Even after I had taken my hand out of my pocket, she was still watching the note, though it was in my pocket behind a comb, beside a wadded up candybar wrapper. I would have bet that she could have told me what kind of candybar wrapper it was.

I saw Lee Mellon the next day. He came over to the city. It had taken him nine hours to hitch-hike from Oakland to San Francisco. He looked pretty grubby. I told him about

the Susan business, about the importance she had placed on
seeing him. I told him that she acted and looked pregnant.
Was, for my opinion.

"That's the way it goes." Lee Mellon said without any
emotion. "I can't do anything about it. I'm hungry. Do
you have anything to eat around here? A sandwich, an egg,
some spaghetti or something? Anything?"

Lee Mellon never mentioned Susan to me again, and I
of course never brought up the subject again. He stayed
over in Oakland for a few more months.

He tried to pawn a stolen electric iron over there. He
spent the whole day going from one hock shop to another
hock shop. Nobody wanted it. Lee Mellon watched the iron
slowly change into a one-legged moldy albatross. He left it
on the bench at a bus stop. It was wrapped in newspaper
and looked like some garbage.

Disillusionment over failing to pawn the iron finally
ended his siege of Oakland. The next day he broke camp and
marched back to Big Sur.

The girl continued living at the San Geronimo Hotel.
Because she was so unhappy she kept getting bigger and
bigger like a cross between a mushroom and a goiter.

Everytime she saw me she asked me anxiously if I had
seen Lee Mellon, and I always lied, no. The disappearance
had us all wondering. What else could I say? Poor girl. So
I lied breathlessly . . . no.

I lied no again no no no no no no no no no no no no no
no no no no no again. I again no no no no no no no no no no
no no no no no Lee Mellon. He has just vanished from the
face of the earth.

Her father, the Freezer King of Sepulveda Boulevard,
disowned her. He argued in the beginning for one of those
Tijuana abortions that have a fancy office and an operating
room clean as a Chevron station. She said no, that she was

going to have the baby. He told her to get out and paid her a monthly stipend never to come back to Los Angeles. When the baby was born, she put it up for adoption.

At the age of seventeen she became quite a character in North Beach. She quickly gained over a hundred pounds. She became huge and grotesque, putting on layers and layers of fat like geological muck.

She decided that she was a painter and being intelligent she realized that it was much easier to talk about painting than to actually paint. So she went to the bars and talked about painters of genius like Van Gogh. There was another painter that she always talked about, but I have forgotten his name.

She also took up smoking cigars and became fanatically anti-German. She smoked cigars and said that all the German men should be castrated slowly, the children buried in snow, and the women set to work in the God-damn salt mines with no other tools than their tears.

Long after she'd had the baby, she would come up to me, waddle up to me is the right way of stating it, and ask if I ever saw Lee Mellon around. I would always say no, and after while it became a joke between us because she knew I had been lying, and by now she herself had seen Lee Mellon, found out the score, and didn't give a damn any more, but she still asked me, "Have you seen Lee Mellon around?" but now *she* was lying. Our positions had been reversed. "No. I haven't," I could say truthfully now.

She went on a kick of having babies for a few years. She turned herself into a baby factory. There's always someone who will go to bed with a fat broad. She gave the babies up for adoption as soon as they were born. It was something to do with her time, and then she grew tired of this, too.

I think by now she was twenty-one, prehistoric, and her fad as a character in North Beach had run its course. She had stopped going to the bars and talking about painters of genius and those bad Germans. She even gave up smoking cigars. She was attending movies all the time now.

She wheeled those by now comfortable layers of fat into the movies every day, taking four or five pounds of food in with her in case there should be a freak snowstorm inside the movie and the concession stand were to freeze solid like the Antarctic.

Once I was standing on a street corner talking to Lee Mellon and she came up to me. "Have you seen Lee Mellon?" she lied with a big smile on her face.

"No," I could say truthfully now.

Lee Mellon didn't show any interest at all in our little game. He said, "The light's changed." He was wearing a gray uniform and his sword rattled as we walked across the street.

Part Two

Campaigning with Lee Mellon
at Big Sur

The Letters of Arrival and Reply

The Letters of Arrival

1

Lee Mellon
General Delivery
Big Sur
California

Dear Lee Mellon,

How are things at Big Sur? Things in San Francisco
are terrible. I have found out rather painfully that love
moves mysteriously through the ways of the stomach, almost
like bees, but the game has turned sour like the bees Isaac
Babel writes about in *Red Cavalry*.

Those bees did not know what to do after their hives
had been blown up by the soldiers. "The Sacred Republic of

51

the Bees" was reduced to nothing but anarchy and tatters.
The bees circled and died in the air.

That's what's happening in my stomach, a rather torn
landscape. I'm looking for a way out. Please excuse this
rather maudlin letter, but I'm in bad shape.

Yours,

Jesse

The Reply

1

Great! Why don't you come down here? I haven't got
any clothes on, and I just saw a whale. There's plenty of
room for everybody. Bring something to drink. Whiskey!
—— As always, Lee Mellon.

The Letters of Arrival

2

Lee Mellon
General Delivery
Big Sur
California

Dear Lee Mellon,

I'm in love with this girl and it is just plain hell with
onions on it. I certainly would like to go down to Big Sur.
I've never been there before.

What's this about your not having any clothes on, and
the whale?

Yours,

Jesse

The Reply

2

Just what I said—no clothes on and a God-damn whale! Can't you smell that sweet sagebrush-by-the-ocean air of Big Sur? Have you no feelings, sir? Do I have to draw you a nostril picture? Tell the broad to take a flying at the moon and come down here with that whiskey and let's catch some abalone and piss off a cliff. —— As always, Lee Mellon

The Letters of Arrival

3

Lee Mellon
General Delivery
Big Sur
California

Dear Lee Mellon,

I've got to get rid of this girl. It just isn't any good. She has drifted over from my stomach to attack my liver.

Is there any shelter down there against the elements? I mean, is there a roof over your head, fella?

Yours,

Jesse

The Reply

3

Oh, shit! Don't make a martyr out of yourself. You know what my philosophy about women is—fuckem/ shuckem. Sure there's God-damn shelter down here. What do you think I'm living in, a burrow? That business in Oakland was something else. A man needs the proper atmosphere to read the Russians. There are four houses down here and only one Lee Mellon. This morning I saw a coyote walking through the sagebrush right at the very edge of the ocean—next stop China. The coyote was acting like he was in New Mexico or Wyoming, except that there were whales passing below. That's what this country does for you. Come down to Big Sur and let your soul have some room to get outside its marrow. —— As always, Lee Mellon

The Letters of Arrival

4

Lee Mellon
General Delivery
Big Sur
California

Dear Lee Mellon,

There are no words to describe the grief this girl is causing me. She's been at it all week.

"The Sacred Republic of the Bees" flows off toward the sea.

I never thought this would happen to me. I feel hopelessly lost. Do any of those cabins have stoves in them?

Yours,

Jesse

The Reply

4

Sure they have stoves! Everyone of them has a dozen stoves. Make up your mind about that broad. Don't let her tan your balls and make a wallet out of them. Just tell her to take a flying at the moon, and tell her you're going down to Big Sur to let your soul rejoice in its freedom in the coyote camp. Tell her you're going to live in a cabin that has a dozen stoves that all burn whiskey until heaven freezes over. —— As always, Lee Mellon

The Letters of Arrival

5

Lee Mellon
General Delivery
Big Sur
California

Dear Lee Mellon,

The girl and I are patching things up. These last few days have been delightful. Perhaps I'll bring her down with me when I go to Big Sur.

Her name is Cynthia. I think you'd really like her.

By the way, your last letter shows strong evidence of a budding literary style.

Yours,

Jesse

The Reply

5

Literary style up your style! My stomach is full of deer steak, biscuits and gravy. Cynthia? Come off it, asshole! Cynthia? You've been writing these crybaby epistles about Cynthia? You really think I'd like Cynthia, huh? I can see it all now—Cynthia? Yes, Lee? It's your turn to slop the abalone. Is it really my turn, Lee? (Fear and disgust in her voice.) Yes, Cynthia, the abalone are calling. They need slopping. Oh, Lee! No! No! No! —— As always, Lee Mellon

The Letters of Arrival

6

Lee Mellon
General Delivery
Big Sur
California

Dear Lee Mellon,

I don't know why you are bitter about Cynthia. You've never even met her before. She is actually quite a girl and would easily adapt herself to any kind of life, besides, what's wrong with the name Cynthia? No kidding, I think you'd really like her.

Yours,

Jesse

The Reply

6

I'm positive I would like her! After all ¾ of the English teachers, ⅔ of the librarians and ½ of the society dames in America are named Cynthia. What's another Cynthia more or less, you poor fart-up. The frogs are croaking in the frog pond. I'm writing by lantern because there is no electricity down here. The wires stop five miles away and I think it's nice of them. Who needs electricity anyway? I did OK in Oakland without electricity. I read Dostoevsky, Turgenev, Gogol, Tolstoy—the Russians. Who needs electricity, but remember when you come down here don't forget to bring Cynthia. I can hardly wait to meet her. Does she have a small mustache? I met a librarian once who was from BM, Battle Mountain, Nevada, that is. She had a small mustache and her name was Cynthia. She came all the way to San Francisco on the bus to give her cherry to a genuine poet. She found one, too. Me! Who knows, it might be the same broad. Ask her something about Battle Mountain, to tell the secrets of BM, like *BM Anthology*. BM! BM! —— As always, Lee Mellon

The Letters of Arrival

7

Lee Mellon
General Delivery
Big Sur
California

Dear Lee Mellon,

The most horrible thing in my life has just happened. I never thought that I would be saying this. Cynthia has left me.

What am I going to do? She's gone for keeps this time. She flew back to Ketchikan this morning.

I'm totally crushed. It just goes to prove that it's never too late to learn. I wonder what that means?

                              Yours,

                                   Jesse

The Reply

7

Cheer up, smarts! You've still got old Lee Mellon and a cabin waiting for you down here at Big Sur. A good cabin. It's on a cliff high over the Pacific. It has a stove and three glass walls. You can lie in bed in the morning and watch the sea otters making it. Very educational. It's the greatest place in the world. What did I tell you about Cynthia? She was probably from Battle Mountain by way of Ketchikan. Weigh well the words of an old campaigner.—A Cynthia in

the library is better than two Cynthias in the sack. ——
As always, Lee Mellon

The Letters of Arrival

8

Lee Mellon
General Delivery
Big Sur
California

Dear Lee Mellon,

No word from Cynthia. All the bees in my stomach are
dead and getting used to it.

This is the end. So be it.

How do we keep alive at Big Sur? I've got a few bucks,
but is there any way to work down there, or what?

Yours,

Jesse

The Reply

8

I've got a garden that grows all year round! A 30:30
Winchester for deer, a .22 for rabbits and quail. I've got
some fishing tackle and *The Journal of Albion Moonlight*.
We can make it OK. What do you want, a fur-lined box of
Kleenex to absorb the sour of your true love Cynthia, the
Ketchikan and/or Battle Mountain cookie? Come to the
party and hurry down to Big Sur and don't forget to bring
some whiskey. I need whiskey!

"Want to put another log on the fire?" Lee Mellon said. "I think it could use another log. What do you think?"

I looked at the fire. I thought about it. Perhaps I thought about it a little too long. The days at Big Sur can do that to you. "Yeah, it looks like it could," I said, and went around to the other end of the cabin and walked through the hole in the kitchen wall and got a log from the pile.

The log was damp and buggy on the bottom. I came back through the hole in the kitchen wall and put the log in the fireplace.

Some bugs hurried to the top of the log and I banged my head hard on the ceiling. "It takes a little while to get used to that," Lee Mellon said, pointing at the 5' 1" ceiling. The bugs were standing there on the log and looking out at us through the fire.

Yes . . . yes, the ceiling. Lee Mellon had been responsible for the ceiling. I'd heard the story. Three bottles of gin and they built the cabin right off the side of the hill, so that one wall of the cabin was just dirt. The fireplace had been carved out of the hillside later and filled in with rocks brought up the cliff from the ocean.

It had been a hot day when they put the walls up and three bottles of gin and Lee Mellon kept putting it away and the other guy, a deeply disturbed religious sort of person, kept putting it away. It was of course his gin, his land, his building material, his mother, his inheritance, and Lee Mellon said, "We've dug the holes deep enough, but the posts are a little too long. I'll saw them off."

Then you begin to get the picture. Four words to be exact. I'll saw them off. But the guy said all right because he was deeply disturbed. Sun, gin, the blue sky and the reflection of the Pacific Ocean were spinning in his addled brain: *Sure, let old Lee Mellon saw them off. No use . . .*

anyway, it's too hot . . . can't fight it, and the cabin had a
5′ 1″ ceiling and no matter how small you were, BANG!
you hit your head against the ceiling.

After a while it became amusing to watch people bang
their heads against the ceiling. Even after you had been
there for a long time, there was no way of getting used to the
ceiling. It existed beyond human intelligence and coordina-
tion. The only victory came from moving around in there
slowly so that when you did hit your head against the ceiling,
the shock of the blow was reduced to minor significance.
That must be some law of physics. It probably has a nice
tongue-bottled name. *The bugs were standing there on the
log looking out at us through the fire.*

Lee Mellon was sitting on a rather mangy-looking deer
rug, leaning up against a board wall. It is important that
one differentiate right now between the walls of the place,
for the walls were of varied and dangerous materials.

There was the dirt wall of the hillside, and there was
a wooden wall, and a glass wall and no wall, just a space of
air that led out to a narrow catwalk that circled part of
the frog pond and joined up with a deck that was canti-
levered rather precariously, like a World War I airplane,
out over a canyon.

Lee Mellon was leaning up against the wooden wall
which was the only wall in the place to bet on. During the
time that I spent down at Big Sur, I saw only one person
lean up against the glass wall. That had been a girl who had
an obsession with going around naked and we took her to
the hospital in Monterey and while she was being sewed
back together again we went down to a hardware store and
got a new sheet of glass. *The bugs were standing there on the
log and looking out at us through the fire.*

And I remember somebody leaning up against the dirt
wall of the hillside, deriding William Carlos Williams, when

suddenly there was a loud roaring, crunching noise and a chunk of the hill fell off and covered the person up to his neck.

The person, being a young classical poet fresh from NYU, began screaming that he was being buried alive. Fortunately, the landslide stopped and we dug him out and dusted him off. That was the last time he said anything against William Carlos Williams. The next day he began reading *Journey to Love* rather feverishly.

I've seen more than one person lean up against the wall that was but a space of air and fall into the frog pond. Usually strong spirits were in rabbit-like evidence whenever this happened.

So the wooden wall was the only safe wall in the place, and Lee Mellon was leaning up against that wall, sitting on a distorted deer rug. It looked as if it had never been tanned, as if after skinning the deer someone took the skin and a pound of garlic and put them together into an oven with a low temperature and left them there for a week or so . . . ugh!

Lee Mellon was rolling a cigarette very carefully. That and leaning up against the wooden wall were the only cautious traits Lee Mellon ever exhibited. *The bugs were standing there on the log and looking out at us through the fire. Bon voyage, bugs. Have a nice trip, little that they could see now.*

I walked out through the wall that was but a space of air to the narrow catwalk and stood there looking down at the frog pond. It was silent because a small amount of the day was still with us, but in a few hours the pond would be changed into the Inquisition. Auto-da-fé at Big Sur. Frogs wearing the robes, carrying the black candles——CROAK! CROAK! CROAK! CROAK!

The frogs would begin at twilight and go all night

long. God-damn them. Frogs, barely the size of quarters. Hundreds, thousands, millions, light years of frogs in that small pond could make enough noise to break one's soul like kindling.

Lee Mellon got up and stood beside me out there on the catwalk. "Soon it will be dark," he said. He stared down at the pond. It looked green and harmless. "I wish I had some dynamite," he said.

Breaking Bread at Big Sur

THE DINNER WE HAD that evening was not very good. How could it be when we were reduced to eating food that the cats would not touch? We had no money to buy anything edible and no prospects of getting any. We were just hanging on.

We had spent four or five days waiting for someone to come along and bring us food, a traveller or a friend, it made no difference. That strange compelling power that draws people to Big Sur had not been working for days.

The switch had been pulled and the Big Sur light turned off for us. That was kind of sad. There was, of course, the same meager traffic along Highway 1, but none of it stopped for us. Something caused them to fall short of us or to continue on beyond us.

I knew that if I ate abalone again I would die. If so much as one more bite of abalone were balanced in my mouth, I knew that my soul would slide out like toothpaste and be diminished for all time in the universe.

We had a little hope that morning but it was quickly

dissipated. Lee Mellon went hunting up on the plateau where the old house was. It was not that he was a bad shot, but that he was excitable. Sometimes there would be doves hanging around the house and quail near a spring where the old man had died years before. Lee Mellon took the last five bullets for the .22 with him. I implored him to take only three. We had quite a discussion about it.

"Save a couple," I said.

"I'm hungry," he said.

"Don't shoot them up in one thrill-crazed flurry," I said.

"I want a quail to eat," Lee Mellon said. "A dove or a big rabbit or a little deer or a pork chop. I'm hungry."

The bullets for the 30:30 had been gone for weeks and everyday, late in the afternoon, the deer would come out on the mountainside. Sometimes there would be twenty or thirty of them, fat and sassy, but we did not have any bullets for the Winchester.

Lee Mellon could not get close enough to do any appreciable damage with the .22. He shot a doe in the ass and the doe limped off into the lilac bushes and got away.

Anyway, I implored him to save a couple of the .22 bullets for a rainy day. "Maybe tomorrow morning we'll find a deer in the garden," I said. Lee Mellon would have none of it. I might as well have been talking about the poems of Sappho.

He went up the mountain to the plateau. There was an awkward dirt road. He kept getting smaller and smaller on the road and our five .22 bullets kept getting smaller and smaller, too. I imagined the bullets now to be about the size of undernourished amoebas. The road switched back behind a grove of redwood trees, and Lee Mellon was no more, taking with him all the bullets we had in the world.

Having nothing better to do, nowhere else to go, I sat

down on a rock beside the highway and waited for Lee Mellon. I had a book with me, something about the soul. The book said everything was all right if you didn't die while you were reading the book, if your fingers maintained life while turning the pages. I approached it as a mystery novel.

Two cars came by. One of the cars had some young people in it. The girl was attractive. I imagined that they had left Monterey at daybreak after having eaten a great big breakfast at the Greyhound bus depot. But that did not quite make sense.

Why would they want to eat breakfast at the Greyhound bus depot? The more I thought about it, the more it seemed unlikely. There were other places to eat breakfast in Monterey. Perhaps some of them were fancier. Just because I had eaten breakfast one morning at the Greyhound bus depot in Monterey did not necessarily mean that everybody in the world ate there.

The second car was a chauffeur-driven Rolls Royce with an old woman sitting in the back seat. She was drenched in furs and diamonds as if wealth had been a sudden spring shower that covered her with all these things instead of rain. How fortunate she was.

She seemed a little surprised at seeing me sitting there like a ground squirrel on a rock. She said something to the chauffeur and his window drifted effortlessly down.

"How far is it to Los Angeles?" he said. His voice was perfect.

Then her window drifted effortlessly down like the neck of a transparent swan. "We're hours late," she said. "But I always wanted to see Big Sur. How far is it to Los Angeles, young man?"

"It's quite a ways to Los Angeles from here," I said. "Hundreds of miles. The road goes slowly until you get to

San Luis Obispo. You should have taken 99 or 101 if you were in a hurry."

"It's too late," she said. "I'll just tell them what happened. They'll understand. Do you have a telephone?"

"No, I'm sorry," I said. "We don't even have electricity."

"It's just as well," she said. "Having them worry a little bit about Granny will be good for them. They've been taking me for granted about ten years now. It'll do them a world of good. I should have thought of it sooner."

I liked the way she said Granny, for the last thing in this world she looked like was somebody's granny.

Then she said thank you in a pleasant way and the windows drifted effortlessly up and the swans resumed their migration south. She waved good-bye and they went down the road and around a bend to the people waiting in Los Angeles, to the people getting more nervous with each passing moment. It probably would be a good thing if they worried about her some.

Where is she? Where is she? Should we call the police? No, let's wait five more minutes.

Five minutes later I heard the dim crack of the .22 and then I heard it again, and still a third time. What a terrible shame it was that we had a repeating rifle—again and again, and then silence.

I waited and Lee Mellon came down off the mountain. He followed the dirt road down and came across the highway. He was carrying the gun rather sloppily, as if it were reduced to the impotence of a stick.

"Well?" I said.

Toward the end of the afternoon Lee Mellon got up and stood beside me out there on the catwalk. "Soon it will be dark," he said. He stared down at the pond. It looked green and harmless. "I wish I had some dynamite," he said. Then he went up to the garden and cut some greens for the salad. When he came back down there was a sort of wistful expression on his face. "I saw a rabbit in the garden," he said.

With an enormous amount of self-control I drove the word Alice away from my mouth and finally out of my mind. I really wanted to say, "What's wrong, Alice, no guts?" but I forced myself to accept the fact that those five bullets were beyond recall.

The dinner we had that evening was not very good. Some salad made from greens and jack mackerel. The fellow who owned the place had brought the jack mackerel for the cats who hung around there, but the cats wouldn't eat it. The stuff was so bad that they would sooner go hungry. And they did.

Jack mackerel tears your system apart. Almost as soon as it hits your stomach, you begin to rumble and squeal and flap. Sounds made in a haunted house during an earthquake tear horizontally across your stomach. Then great farts and belches begin arriving out of your body. Jack mackerel almost comes out through the pores.

After a dinner of jack mackerel you sit around and your subjects of conversation are greatly limited. I have found it impossible to talk about poetry, esthetics or world peace after eating jack mackerel.

To make the meal a perfect gastronomical Hiroshima, we had some of Lee Mellon's bread for dessert. His bread fits perfectly the description of hardtack served to the soldiers of the Civil War. But that, of course, is no surprise.

I had learned to hold my face at absolute attention, my eyes saluting a silent flag, the flag of the one who does the cooking, when every few days, Lee Mellon would say, "I guess it's time to bake some more bread."

It had taken a little while, but I had gotten so I could eat it now: Hard as a rock, flavorless and an inch thick, like Betty Crocker gone to hell, or thousands of soldiers marching along a road in Virginia, taking up miles of the countryside.

Preparing for Ecclesiastes

A LITTLE WHILE AFTER DINNER, to avoid the sound of the frogs that were really laying it in now from the early color of the evening, I decided to take my farts and belches to the privacy of my cabin and read Ecclesiastes.

"I think I'm going to sit here and read frogs," Lee Mellon farted.

"What did you say, Lee? I can't hear you. The frogs. Yell louder," I farted.

Lee Mellon got up and threw a great big rock into the pond and screamed, "Campbell's Soup!" The frogs were instantly quiet. That would work for a few moments and then they would start in again. Lee Mellon had quite a pile of rocks in the room. The frogs would always begin with one croak, and then the second and then the 7,452nd frog would join in.

Funny thing though, about Lee Mellon's yelling "Campbell's Soup!" at the frogs while he was launching various missiles into the pond. He had yelled every kind

70

of obscenity possible at them, and then he decided to experiment with nonsense syllables to see if they would have any effect, along with a well-aimed rock.

Lee Mellon had an inquiring mind and by the hit-or-miss method he came upon "Campbell's Soup!" as the phrase that struck the most fear into the frogs. So now, instead of yelling some boring obscenity, he yelled, "Campbell's Soup!" at the top of his voice in the Big Sur night.

"Now what did you say?" I farted.

"I think I'm going to sit here and read frogs. What's wrong, don't you like frogs?" Lee Mellon farted. "That's what I said. Where's your spirit of patriotism? After all, there's a frog on the American flag."

"I'm going to my cabin," I farted. "Read some Ecclesiastes."

"You've been reading a lot of Ecclesiastes lately," Lee Mellon farted. "And as I remember there's not that much to read. Better watch yourself, kid."

"Just putting in time," I said.

"I think dynamite's too good for these frogs," Lee Mellon said. "I'm working on something special. Dynamite's too fast. I'm getting a great idea."

Lee Mellon had tried various ways of silencing the frogs. He had thrown rocks at them. He had beaten the pond with a broom. He had thrown pans full of boiling water on them. He had thrown two gallons of sour red wine into the pond.

For a time he was catching the frogs when they first appeared at twilight and throwing them down the canyon. He caught a dozen or so every evening and vanquished them down the canyon. This went on for a week.

Lee Mellon suddenly got the idea that they were

crawling back up the canyon again. He said that it took them a couple of days. "God-damn them," he said. "It's a long pull up, but they're making it."

He'd gotten so mad that the next frog he caught he threw into the fireplace. The frog became black and stringy and then the frog became not at all. I looked at Lee Mellon. He looked at me. "You're right. I'll try something else."

He took a couple dozen rocks and spent an afternoon tying pieces of string to them, and then that evening when he caught the frogs, he tied them to the rocks and threw them down the canyon. "That ought to slow them down a little bit. Make it a little harder to get back up here," he said, but it did not work out for there were just too many frogs to fight effectively, and after another week he grew tired of this and went back to throwing rocks at the pond and shouting "Campbell's Soup!"

At least we never saw any frogs in the pond with rocks tied to their backs. That would have been too much.

There were a couple of little water snakes in the pond, but they could only eat a frog or two every day or so. The snakes weren't very much help. We needed anacondas. The snakes we had were more ornamental than functional.

"Well, I'll leave you to the frogs," I farted. The first one had just croaked and now they would all start up again and hell would come forth from that pond.

"Mark my words, Jesse. I got a plan going," Lee Mellon farted and then tapped his head with his finger in the fashion people do to see if a watermelon is ripe. It was. A shiver traveled down my spine.

"Good-night," I farted.

"Yes, indeed," Lee Mellon farted.

The Rivets in Ecclesiastes

I WENT UP to my cabin. I could hear the ocean below banging against the rocks. I passed the garden. It was covered with fishnets to keep the birds off.

As usual I stumbled over the motorcycle that was beside my bed. The motorcycle was one of Lee Mellon's pets. It was lying there in about forty-five parts.

A couple of times every week, Lee Mellon would say, "I think I'll put my motorcycle together. It's a four-hundred-dollar motorcycle." He always said that it was a four-hundred-dollar motorcycle, but nothing ever came of it.

I lit the lantern and was enclosed within the glass walls of the cabin. My place was furnished like all the other cabins down there. I did not have a table, any chairs or a bed.

I slept on the floor in a sleeping bag and used two white rocks for bookends. I used the engine block of the motorcycle to set the lantern on, so I could raise the light to make reading a little more comfortable.

The cabin had a very crude wood stove, Lee Mellon's

creation, that could warm the place up instantly on a cold night, but the moment you did not put another piece of wood in the stove, the cabin would be plunged right back into the cold.

I was, of course, reading Ecclesiastes at night in a very old Bible that had heavy pages. At first I read it over and over again every night, and then I read it once every night, and then I began reading just a few verses every night, and now I was just looking at the punctuation marks.

Actually I was counting them, a chapter every night. I was putting the number of punctuation marks down in a notebook, in neat columns. I called the notebook "The Punctuation Marks in Ecclesiastes." I thought it was a nice title. I was doing it as a kind of study in engineering.

Certainly before they build a ship they know how many rivets it takes to hold the ship together and the various sizes of the rivets. I was curious about the number of rivets and the sizes of those rivets in Ecclesiastes, a dark and beautiful ship sailing on our waters.

A summary of my little columns would go something like this: the first chapter of Ecclesiastes has 57 punctuation marks and they are broken down into 22 commas, 8 semicolons, 8 colons, 2 question marks and 17 periods.

The second chapter of Ecclesiastes has 103 punctuation marks and they are broken down into 45 commas, 12 semicolons, 15 colons, 6 question marks and 25 periods.

The third chapter of Ecclesiastes has 77 punctuation marks and they are broken down into 33 commas, 21 semicolons, 8 colons, 3 question marks and 12 periods.

The fourth chapter of Ecclesiastes has 58 punctuation marks and they are broken down into 25 commas, 9 semicolons, 5 colons, 2 question marks and 17 periods.

The fifth chapter of Ecclesiastes has 67 punctuation

marks and they are broken down into 25 commas, 7 semicolons, 15 colons, 3 question marks and 17 periods.

And this is what I was doing by lantern light at Big Sur, and I gained a pleasure and an appreciation by doing this. Personally I think the Bible gains by reading it with a lantern. I do not think the Bible has ever truly adjusted to electricity.

By lantern light, the Bible shows its best. I counted the punctuation marks in Ecclesiastes very carefully so as not to make a mistake, and then I blew the lantern out.

Begging for Their Lives

AROUND MIDNIGHT OR AN HOUR LATER—this is just a guess for we had no clocks at Big Sur—I heard some noises in my sleep. They came from the old truck we had parked up by the highway. The noises kept renewing themselves and then I could tell they were human sounds but there was a muttering and a strangeness to them and then a voice yelled, "For God's sake please don't shoot me!"

I unzipped myself from the sleeping bag and put my pants on very quickly. I found a small ax in the dark and wondered what the hell was happening out there. There was a lot of noise and none of it was pleasant. I went out carefully, moving with the shadows for I didn't want to just stumble out there and get fucked if that's what was happening out there. I was going to take it nice and easy, like they do in the Western movies.

I moved cautiously toward the sounds and the voices. A voice, the calmest one, belonged to Lee Mellon. There was

76

a lantern on the ground and now I could see what was happening. I stopped in the shadows.

There were two guys on their knees in front of Lee Mellon. They were kids, probably teen-agers. Lee Mellon stood over them with the Winchester. He was holding it in an extremely businesslike manner.

"Please, for God's sake . . . please, please we didn't know, please," one of them said. They were both wearing very nice clothes. Lee Mellon stood there in front of them, wearing rags.

Lee Mellon was talking to them very quietly and calmly, perhaps as John Donne delivered his sermons in Elizabethan times. "I can shoot you fellas right through the heads like dogs and throw your bodies down there to the sharks and then drive your car down to Cambria. Wipe my fingerprints off. Leave the car there, and no one will ever know what happened to you. The sheriff's car will drive up and down the highway for a few days. The sheriff will stop here and ask some silly questions. I'll reply, 'No, I haven't seen them down this way, Sheriff.' Then they will drop the whole business, and you'll both be filed away permanently in the missing persons section in Salinas. I hope you fellas don't have any mothers, girl friends or pets because they're not going to see you for a long, long time."

One of them was crying very hard. He did not have the power of speech. The other one was crying too, but he could still talk. "Please, please, please, please, please," he said as if he were repeating a nursery rhyme.

It was then that I walked out of the shadows with the ax in my hand. I thought that they were both going to shit right there and ooze straight through to China.

"Howdy, Jesse," Lee Mellon said. "Look what I got here. A couple of smart fuckers, trying to syphon our gas. Guess what, Jesse?"

"What's up, Lee?" I said.

Do you see how perfect our names were, how the names lent themselves to this kind of business? Our names were made for us in another century.

"I think I'm going to kill them, Jesse," Lee Mellon said calmly. "I've got to start someplace. This is the third time in the last month somebody's come down here and stolen our gas. I've got to start someplace. Can't let this go on forever. Jesse, I think I'll take these two shit fuckers for a down payment and shoot them."

Lee Mellon took the barrel of the empty Winchester and placed it against the forehead of the one who could still talk, and then he could not talk any more. The power of speech had fled his mouth. He made all the motions of talking, but there wasn't anything coming out.

"Wait a minute, Lee." I said. "Sure, these guys need shooting. Steal a man's gas down here in the wilderness, leave him up shit creek without even a pair of roller skates. They deserve being shot, but they're only a couple of young kids. Look, barely out of high school. See that peach fuzz."

Lee Mellon bent down and sort of looked at their chins.

"Yeah, Jesse," Lee Mellon said. "I know. But we got a pregnant woman down there in the cabin. My wife, that's my wife down there, and I love her. She's ready to have a baby at any time. She's two weeks over. We'd come up here, get in the truck to take her to Monterey so she could have a doctor and a nice clean hospital, and then there wouldn't be any gas in the truck and the baby would die.

"No, Jesse, no—no, no," Lee Mellon said. "For killing my baby son, I think I'd better shoot them now. Hell, I can make them put their heads together and use just one bullet. I got a slow one here. Take about five minutes to go through their heads. Hurt like hell."

The one who had never been able to say anything from

the moment Lee Mellon had stepped out there with the lantern and the gun, and told them if they moved one inch he would kill them, but they might as well move because he was going to kill them anyway, and liked a running target because it sharpened his eye—finally spoke, "I'm nineteen. We couldn't even find the gas tank. My sister lives in Santa Barbara." That was all he said, and his tongue was gone again. They were both crying very hard. The tears were coming down their cheeks and their noses were running.

"Yeah," Lee Mellon said. "They are young, Jesse. I guess a person should have a second chance before they get their fucking brains blown out for trying to steal gasoline from a baby that hasn't even been born yet." When he said that, they both started crying harder than ever, if that were possible.

"Well, Lee," I said. "No harm done. Nothing has really happened except that they tried to steal our last five gallons of gasoline."

"All right, Jesse," Lee Mellon said philosophically, though dragging his feet a little. "If they pay for all the gasoline they've been stealing from us this month, I might let them live. Just might. I once promised my mother, God bless her soul in heaven above, that if I ever had the chance to give a helping hand to some wayward boys, I would. How much money do you boys have?"

Both of them instantly, without saying anything, like a pair of mute Siamese twins, took out their wallets and gave Lee Mellon all of their money. They had about $6.72.

Lee Mellon took the money and put it in his pocket. "You boys have shown faith," he said. "You can live." One of them crawled forward and kissed Lee Mellon's boot.

"Come on, now," Lee Mellon said. "Don't slobber. Show some class." He marched them back to their car. They were the happiest kids in the world. Their car was a 1941

Ford with all those good things kids do that make them look nice.

The kids had probably been low on gas, taken the wrong road. They should have been over on 101. With no filling station for miles and miles, they decided that we wouldn't miss a few gallons of gas. They probably would have asked us if there had been a light on.

Lee Mellon waved good-bye with the Winchester as they drove off very slowly toward San Luis Obispo and the sister waiting in Santa Barbara. Yeah, it was probably just a mistake in navigation. They should have stayed over on 101.

Lee Mellon waved good-bye with the Winchester and at the same time, he pulled the trigger of the gun. They were, of course, too far away now to hear the gun go off. They were maybe fifty yards away, the car barely rolling forward, and they couldn't possibly have heard the click of the hammer as it hit against the empty chamber.

The Truck

THE NEXT MORNING we had cracked wheat for breakfast. We had a fifty-pound sack of it that had been bought in San Francisco at the old Crystal Palace Market. This was in the days before they tore that lovely building down and put a motel in there.

Cracked wheat was our lonesome breakfast when the food ran low. We had some powdered milk to go along with it, and some sugar and some of Lee Mellon's hardtack. There was no coffee, so we had some green tea.

"Well, we're rich," Lee Mellon said, taking the $6.72 out of his pocket. He put the money down on the floor in front of him like a coin collector looking at some rare specimens.

"We can get some food," I said naïvely. "And maybe some bullets for the guns."

"I wonder if those guys will ever get the stains out of their pants," Lee Mellon laughed. "It's for sure they won't take them to the cleaners."

"Ha-ha," I laughed.

One of the cats jumped down off the roof. We had about half-a-dozen cats. They were all starving. The cat came over and tried to eat a piece of Lee Mellon's hardtack. It took a few gnaws and decided that it wasn't worth the effort.

The cat went out on the deck and sat there in the weak sun, and watched a snake gliding pleasantly across the pond with a half-digested frog in its tummy.

"Let's take this money and get laid," Lee Mellon said. "I think that's more important than food or bullets. I did all right without bullets. We ought to move that truck a little closer to the highway. It might eventually lead to a good living."

"How do you get laid for $6.72?" I asked.

"We'll go up and see Elizabeth."

"I thought she only worked when she was in Los Angeles," I said.

"Yeah, that's the way she usually does it, but sometimes she doesn't mind. To be different. You have to catch her in the right mood. What she does down in Los Angeles is kind of weird stuff."

"A box of .22 bullets would be really sweet," I said. "A pound of coffee . . . both of us? A hundred dollar Los Angeles call girl for $6.72? You're awake, aren't you, fella?"

"Sure," he said. "I think it might be OK. Anyway, we haven't got anything to lose. Maybe she'll invite us for breakfast. Finish that slice of bread and let's get going."

What a wonderful sense of distortion Lee Mellon had. Finish that slice of bread. That thing I was holding in my hand had never had anything to do with a slice of bread. I put my hammer and chisel aside and we went up to the truck.

The truck looked just like a Civil War truck if they'd

had trucks back in those times. But the truck ran, even though it didn't have a gas tank.

There was an empty fifty-gallon gasoline drum on the bed of the truck with a smaller gasoline can on top of it, and there was a syphon leading from that can to the fuel line.

It worked like this. Lee Mellon drove and I stayed on the back of the truck and made sure everything went all right with the syphon, that it didn't get knocked out of kilter by the motion of the truck.

We looked kind of funny going down the highway. I'd never had the heart to ask Lee Mellon what happened to the gas tank. I figured it was best not to know.

In the Midst of Life

I HAD MET ELIZABETH only a couple of times, but I had been very impressed. She was beautiful and worked in Los Angeles three months out of the year. She hired somebody, usually a Mexican woman, to come to Big Sur and watch her children. Then she performed a fantastic change and did it with great skill.

At Big Sur she lived in a rough three-room shack with four children that were all reflections of herself as if she had hung mirrors on them. She wore her hair long and loose about her shoulders and on her feet she wore sandals and on her body she wore a rough shapeless dress and lived a life of physical and spiritual contemplation.

She had her garden and her canning and chopping wood and sewing and she did all the things that women have always done when there is not a man about the house and they live in the lonely reaches of the world, raising the children as best they can. She was very gentle and read a lot.

She lived this life for nine months out of the year, like

some strange pregnancy, and then she hired somebody to watch her children, and she went to Los Angeles and made the physical and spiritual transformation into a hundred dollar call girl who specialized in providing exotic pleasure for men who wanted a beautiful woman to put out with some weird action.

She did all the things that the men wanted her to do. They gave her the hundred dollars and sometimes more because she was very comfortable and did not make them feel self-conscious about what they wanted, not unless the men wanted to be made uncomfortable, of course, and then she would do this relentlessly and sometimes they paid her extra for making them feel so uncomfortable.

She was a highly paid technician who worked three months out of the year, saving the money. Then she went back to Big Sur and let her hair hang long and naturally about her neck and shoulders, and she lived a life of physical and spiritual contemplation and could not stand to kill a living thing.

She was a vegetarian. Eggs were her only vice. There were rattlesnakes around where her children played, but she would do nothing about it.

Her oldest child was eleven and her youngest six, and the rattlesnakes were in abundance. The snakes came and went like mice, but her children remained unaltered by them.

Her husband had been killed in Korea. That's all that anybody knew about him. She came to Big Sur after his death. She didn't care to talk about it.

We drove up to her place. It was about twelve miles away, and then off the highway a few miles up an obscure canyon. You had to watch carefully. It was easy to miss her road. Our maximum speed on the highway was twenty miles an hour. When we reached her place we stopped the truck and Lee Mellon got out and I got off. We made quite a team.

There was a long line of clothes between two trees. They hung perfectly still for there was no wind. We could see children's toys here and there, and we saw a game that the children had made themselves out of dirt, deer antlers and abalone shells, but the game was so strange that only children could tell what it was. Perhaps it wasn't a game at all, only the grave of a game.

Elizabeth's car was gone. Everything was quiet except for some chickens in a pen. A rooster was strutting around making a bunch of noise. Nobody was home.

Lee Mellon looked at the rooster. He decided to steal it, and then he decided to leave her some money for it along with a note on the kitchen table telling her that he had bought the chicken, and then he decided to hell with it. Let her keep the chicken. That was big of him. And all the time that this was going on, it was going on only in his mind, for he did not say a word.

Finally Lee Mellon did speak, saying, "Nobody's home," and that was right except for a rooster destined to live forever and the grave of a children's game.

The Extremity of $6.72

WHEN WE ARRIVED BACK at our place and Lee Mellon got out and I got off the truck, I could see that thirst had built itself a kind of shack in Lee Mellon's throat. Thoughts of strong drink crossed his eyes like birds in flight.

"I wish she had been home," Lee Mellon said, picking up a rock and throwing it at the Pacific Ocean. The rock did not quite reach the Pacific. It landed on a pile of about seven billion other rocks.

"Yeah," I said.

"Who knows what might have happened?" Lee Mellon said.

I was quite certain that nothing would have happened, but I said, "Yeah, if she had been home . . ."

The birds kept crossing his eyes, flocks of little drinky-winkies, their wings attached by glass to their bodies. A fog was building up on the ocean. It was not building up like a shack, but more like a grand hotel. The Grand Hotel of Big Sur. Soon it would start inward and curve up the slope of the canyon and everything would be lost in flocks of vaporous bellboys.

Lee Mellon was getting pretty nervous. "Let's hitchhike to Monterey and get drunk," he said.

"Only if I can fill my pockets with rice when we get there, and put a pound of hamburger in my wallet before we start drinking," I said. I used the word wallet like one uses the word mausoleum.

"OK," he said.

Eight hours later I was sitting in a small bar in Monterey with a young girl. She had a glass of red wine in front of her and I had a martini in front of me. Sometimes it just happens that way. There's no telling the future and little understanding of what's gone on before. Lee Mellon was passed out underneath the saloon. I had hosed the vomit off him and covered him with a large piece of cardboard so the police wouldn't find him.

There were a lot of other people in the bar. At first I could barely contain my amusement at human and public surroundings. I was pretending very hard that I was a human being and by doing so, I allowed myself to come on with the girl.

I had met her about an hour earlier when Lee Mellon had passed out on top of her. In subtracting him from her, a thing not taught in grade school arithmetic, we had struck up a casual conversation and it had flowered into us sitting opposite each other and having a drink together.

I held a sip of the cold martini in my mouth until the temperature of the drink was the same temperature as my body. The good old 98.6 fahrenheit—our only link with reality. That is if you want to consider a mouth full of martini as having anything to do with reality.

Elaine was the girl's name and the more I watched her the prettier she flowered out, which is a nice thing if one can pull it off. It's hard. She could. That certain acceleration that comes from within has always pleased me.

"What do you do?" she asked.

I had to think that one over. I could have said, "I live with Lee Mellon and I am cursed like a dog." No, no, not that. I could have said, "Do you like apples?" and she would have answered yes, and then I could have said, "Let's go to bed." No, no, that would be later. Finally I decided on what I was going to say to her. I said quietly, but lined with a gentle certainty, "I live in Big Sur."

"Oh, that's nice," she said. "I live in Pacific Grove. What do you do?"

Not bad I thought. I'll try something else.

"I'm unemployed," I said.

"I'm unemployed, too," she said. "What do you do?"

This was a strong new part of her to be dealt with, but I was ready to go now. Let me go! I looked at her very shyly with a sort of religious awkwardness that was stacked like palm branches about me. "I'm a minister," I said.

She looked at me just as shyly and said just as awkwardly, "I'm a nun. What do you do?"

There was a persistence there. We were beginning to hit it off. I liked her. I've always been partial to clever women. It is a weakness of mine, but it's too late to correct.

A little while later we were walking along the beach. I had my arm under her sweater and around her waist and my hand going sideways up to her breast and my fingers doing things, reaching out with the intelligence of small plants that were footloose and fancy-free.

Jesse's got a girl and Lee Mellon introduced her to him. "When did you first decide to go into the nunnery?" I said.

"Oh, when I was about six," she said.

"I decided to be a minister when I was five," I said.

"I decided to be a nun when I was four."

"I decided to be a minister when I was three."

"That's nice. I decided to be a nun when I was two."

"I decided to be a minister when I was one."

"I decided to be a nun the day I was born. That very day. It's good to start your life out on the right foot," she said proudly.

"Well, I wasn't there when I was born so I couldn't make the decision. My mother was in Bombay. I was in Salinas. I think you're being very unfair," I said humbly.

This broke her up. It is pleasant when such silliness can lead to a girl's place. She closed the door and I glanced at her books, a very bad habit of mine. Hello, *Collected Poems* of Dylan Thomas. I looked over her place like a raccoon, another habit of mine but not as bad, though.

I have a great curiosity about the abodes where the young ladies live. I like the smells of where the young ladies live and the artifacts and the way the light falls upon things, especially the light upon the smells.

She made me a sandwich. I didn't eat it. I don't know why she made it. We got into bed. I put my hand between her legs. The blanket underneath her had a rodeo on it. Cowboys and horses and corrals. She forced her body hard against my hand.

Just before we went away with each other like small republics to join the United Nations, I had a cinematographic impression, about a dozen frames of Lee Mellon lying covered with cardboard underneath the saloon.

To Gettysburg! To Gettysburg!

AFTER A LONG PLEASANT WHILE I got up and sat on the edge of the bed. There was a small light in the room and an abstract painting coming out of the light. Elaine had a lamp with an abstract painted upon the shade. All right . . .

There was the old standby, that faithful servant of the walls: the Manolete bullfight poster you see again and again upon the wall of the young ladies. How well they like that poster and how it likes them. They take care of each other.

There was a guitar with the word LOVE written on the back, and the strings of the guitar were turned to the wall as if the wall should suddenly begin to plink out a little tune, a few snatches of "Greensleeves" or the "Midnight Special."

"What are you doing?" Elaine said, staring softly at me. Sexual satisfaction had puzzled her face. She was like a child that had just awakened from its nap, though she had never been asleep.

I was pleased with myself for it had been a long time

or seemed so, and pleased I was with myself again, and again pleased to be pleased again.

"I've got to get Lee Mellon out from underneath that saloon," I said. "I don't want the police to get him. He wouldn't like that. Hates jail. Always has. The thrill of jail was ruined for him when he was a child."

"What?" she said.

"Yeah," I said. "He did ten years for murdering his parents."

She pulled the covers up over her body and lay there smiling at me, who in turn was smiling. Then slowly she drifted the covers down to the beginning of her breasts and below them, a thing "infinitely gentle" moving . . . down.

"The police will get Lee Mellon," I said. I said it like a slogan in a socialist country. GUARD AGAINST ELEC-TRICAL WASTE AND TURN THE LIGHTS OUT WHEN YOU LEAVE THE ROOM. THE POLICE WILL GET LEE MELLON. It was all the same. "The police will get Lee Mellon," I repeated.

Elaine smiled and then said all right. It was all right. This life, how strange it is. Last night those two boys were crawling in front of Lee Mellon's empty rifle, little realizing as they begged for their imaginary lives that they were going to finance all of this: I with a girl to the bed, Lee Mellon under a saloon covered with cardboard.

Elaine got out of the bed. "I'll go with you. We can bring him here and sober him up."

She pulled the sweater over the top of her head and then she put her pants on. I was her appreciative Olympian audience, watching things going away into clothes and then appearing again with clothes on top of them. She put on a pair of tennis shoes.

"Who are you?" asked I, the Horatio Alger of Casanovas.

"My parents live in Carmel," she said.

Then she walked over and put her arms around me and kissed me on the mouth. I felt pretty good.

We found Lee Mellon right where I left him, cardboard still intact. He was like a box full of something and it certainly wasn't soap. A great big box full of Lee Mellon had arrived suddenly in America without any advertising campaign.

"Wake up, Lee Mellon," I said and began singing,

Way, hay, up she rises. Way, hay, up she rises,
Way, hay, up she rises earlye in the morning!

What will we do with the drunken general?
What will we do with the drunken general?
What will we do with the drunken general
earlye in the morning?

Why, send him off to Gettysburg!
Off to Gettysburg! To Gettysburg! O Gettysburg
earlye in the morning!

Elaine put her hand down the back of my pants and then slipped her fingers down past my shorts and let her hand go on down to the crack of my ass, and there her hand did rest like a bird upon the branch of a tree.

Lee Mellon slowly sat up. The cardboard fell away from him. He was unpacked. The world could now see him. The end product of American spirit, pride and the old know-how.

"What happened?" he said.

"Spiritus frumenti," Elaine said.

Great Day

THE NEXT MORNING WE DROVE down to Big Sur in Elaine's car. The back seat of the car was filled with sacks of food from the Safeway market in Monterey. There were two alligators in the trunk of the car. They were Elaine's idea.

Lee Mellon had blurted out in a flurry of drunken speech the trouble we'd had with the frogs, and Elaine just as fast but coherently said, "I'll get an alligator," and she did.

She went down to the pet shop and came back with two alligators. We asked her why she'd gotten two alligators, and she said they were on sale. Buy one at the regular price and you got another one for a penny. An alligator one cent sale. In its own way it made sense.

Happiness sagged out of Lee Mellon's bloodshot eyes as he drove while Elaine and I sat beside him in the front seat. I had my arm around her. We drove by Henry Miller's mailbox. He was waiting for his mail in that old Cadillac he had in those days.

"There's Henry Miller," I said.

"Oh," she said.

With every passing moment my liking for her flowered another time. Not that I had anything against Henry Miller, but like a storm of flowers remembered during a revolution I grew to like her more and more.

Lee Mellon was very impressed, too. She had bought fifty dollars worth of food and two alligators. Lee Mellon took his tongue and absentmindedly counted the teeth in his mouth. He found six in there and he divided the six teeth into the sacks of food in the back seat, and he was pleased with his mathematics for a smile like a ragged Parthenon appeared on his face.

"Great day!" Lee Mellon said. That was the first time I'd ever heard him say great day. I'd heard him say everything else but great day. He probably just said it to confuse me. He did.

"I've never been to Big Sur before," Elaine said, looking out the window at the passing country. "My parents moved to Carmel while I was going to college in the East."

"A college girl?" Lee Mellon said, turning suddenly to her as if she had announced that all the food in the back seat wasn't really food but cleverly designed wax.

"Oh, no!" she said triumphantly. "I failed all my courses and they blew up the college the day I left because I was so stupid. They felt the place couldn't be used for anything again."

"Good," Lee Mellon said, resuming visual control of the car.

There was a large bird in the sky. It went out over the ocean, and stayed there.

"This is beautiful," Elaine said.

"Great day!" Lee Mellon repeated to my consternation.

Motorcycle

WE NEARED OUR PLACE late in the afternoon. Half a mile away there was a wooden bridge and a creek that flashed below. I was holding Elaine's hand. Like a bottle of beer in a haze the sun was plying its ancient Egyptian trade toward the end of the sky, the beginning of the Pacific. Lee Mellon was holding the steering wheel of the car. We were all content.

Lee Mellon pulled off the highway and drove up to the old truck and stopped.

"What's that?" Elaine said.

"That's a truck," I said.

"Come off it," she said.

"I made it with my own hands," Lee Mellon said.

"That explains it," Elaine said. In an extraordinarily brief period of time she had grown to know, to understand what went on behind the surface of Lee Mellon. This pleased me.

"Well, here we are," Lee Mellon said. "The Homestead.

My grandpappy homesteaded this place. Fought Indians, drought, floods, cattlemen, varmints, the Southern Pacific, Frank Norris and strong drink. But do you know the worst thing we Mellons had to fight and still have to fight, the thing that finally gets us all?"

"No," Elaine said.

"The Mellon Curse. It comes in the form of a gigantic hound every decade. You know 'Twas not the track of man nor beast, but that of a gigantic Mellon Curse.' "

"Sounds reasonable," she said.

We got the groceries and took them through the hole in the kitchen wall. The cats darted into the brush like books into a library. It would take them a little while but hunger would return them to us like the classics: *Hamlet, Winesburg, Ohio*.

"What about the alligators?" Elaine said.

"Let's save them for tonight. They're OK in the car," Lee Mellon said, as if it were a perfectly natural thing for alligators to be in a car. "I've waited and dreamt of this for months. We'll show those frogs that man is the dominant creature on this shit pile, and they better believe it."

Elaine looked the place over and the light of Big Sur was upon her hair, and her hair was in perfect tune with California. "Very interesting," she said, and then hit her head on the ceiling. I comforted her, but it wasn't necessary. She hadn't hit her head very hard. It was only a love tap compared to some of the bone-crushing smashes I'd seen delivered against those beams.

"Who designed this place?" she said. "Frank Lloyd Wright?"

"No," I said. "Frank Lloyd Mellon."

"Oh, he's an architect, too."

Lee Mellon came over and inspected the ceiling from a kind of weird stoop. He was like a doctor taking the pulse of a dead patient. I looked at myself. I was stooping the same way and Elaine was, too. We were all joined together in the famous Lee Mellon Indoor Stoop, a thing that would have been copyrighted during the Inquisition.

It's a little low," he said to Elaine.

"Yes, it is," I said.

"You'll get used to it," Lee Mellon said to Elaine.

"I'm certain she will," I said.

"I will," she said.

Lee Mellon went and got a bottle of wine from the groceries and we walked out onto the deck and toasted the sundown. The sun broke like a beer bottle on the water. We in a shallow sort of way reflected ourselves in the broken glass of the Egyptians. Each piece of Ra went away with a 60 horsepower Johnson outboard motor fastened to it.

The wine was Wente Brothers gray riesling, soon gone.

"Where do we stay?" Elaine said. I steered her back up to the car and got her suitcase and took her to the glass house, past the garden covered with fishnets.

"What's that?" she said.

"It's a garden covered with fishnets."

We went inside the glass house and she looked at the floor.

"A motorcycle?" she said.

"Sort of," I said.

"Lee Mellon's," she said.

"Yes."

"Uh-huh," nodding her head.

"This place is cosy," she said, dropping her hands to her side. Then she saw the Bible. "You are a minister!"

"Yes, I am. I attended the Moody Bible Institute and studied to be a church janitor. I'm doing graduate work now at Napa State Hospital. Soon I'll have a church of my own. This is my vacation. I come here every year for the waters."

"Uh-huh," nodding her head.

Elaine sat down on the place where I slept and looked up at me, and then she lay carefully back upon the sleeping bag. "This is your bed," she said, not asking a question.

There was no rodeo engraved upon my bed. No horses, no cowboys, no corrals. Nothing but sleeping bag. It seemed a little weird now as if all the places where people sleep in the world should have rodeos upon them.

I looked out the window and Lee Mellon was coming up the path to the house. I took my hand and waved him back. He paused, looked and cocked his head like a Confederate general, and turned around and went back down to the hole in the kitchen wall.

"What's that underneath the lantern?" Elaine said.

"Motorcycle," I said.

A Farewell to Frogs

ELAINE COOKED DINNER THAT EVENING. What a joy it was to have a woman behind the stove. She was our fair queen of grub as she fried up some pork chops. It was then I realized for the first time the extent of the damage Lee Mellon's cooking had done to my soul.

I don't believe I have ever fully healed spiritually from his cooking. I have built defensive mechanisms around those tragic memories, but the pain is still there. If I but for an instant diminish my defenses, the cloven hoof of his bad cooking prances again in all its dubious glory upon my palate.

Lee Mellon built a grandiose fire and we sat around the fire drinking cups of strong black coffee. Elaine had even bought some cat food. The cats were in there with us, stretched out like furry ferns in front of the fire. Everybody was nice and comfy. While the cats purred up from the depths of their prehistoric memories a rusty old plantlike purr—they were so little used to contentment—we engaged in dialogue.

"What do your parents do?" Lee Mellon said paternally. I choked on my coffee.

"I'm their daughter," Elaine said.

Lee Mellon stared blankly at her for a few seconds. "Sounds like a vaguely familiar story. Conan Doyle, I guess. *The Case of the Smart Ass Daughter*," Lee Mellon said.

He went and got one of our brand-new apples out of the kitchen. He began working on it with his six teeth. I knew the apples were crisp but there was no sound coming out of his mouth that would have indicated the presence of that quality.

"My father's a lawyer," Elaine said.

Lee Mellon nodded. There were hand grenade fragments of apple around the corners of his mouth.

Elaine reached over and put her hand on my thigh. I put my arm around her and leaned back against the wooden wall. Lee Mellon was enthroned upon his stale deer hide.

Night was coming on in, borrowing the light. It had started out borrowing just a few cents worth of the light, but now it was borrowing thousands of dollars worth of the light every second. The light would soon be gone, the bank closed, the tellers unemployed, the bank president a suicide.

We sat there quietly watching Lee Mellon valiantly attacking the world's longest apple, and then we were close to each other, and then we went back silently to Lee Mellon and the apple, and then back to ourselves and finally we were not watching the apple masquerade any more but were totally involved within our closeness to each other.

When Lee Mellon finished the apple he smacked his lips together like a pair of cymbals, and we heard the first frog.

"There it goes," Lee Mellon said, preparing immediately to send his cavalry in, dust rising in the valley, an excitment in the time of banners, in the time of drums.

We heard the second frog, and then we heard the first frog over again. A third frog joined in, and then they all had one good one together, and then a fourth frog came on through, and three other frogs popped like firecrackers, and Lee Mellon said, "I'll go get the alligators." He lit a lantern and walked through the hole in the kitchen wall and up the path to the car.

Elaine must have dozed off suddenly. She was lying on the floor with her head on my lap. She was a little startled. "Where's Lee Mellon?" she said. I barely heard her.

"He's gone to get the alligators," I said loudly.

"Are those the frogs?" she said loudly and pointing toward the noise that was beginning to boil all over the dark pond.

"Yes," I said loudly.

"Good," she said loudly.

Lee Mellon came back with the alligators. He had a nice six-toothed smile on his face. He put the box down and took one of the alligators out. The alligator was stunned to realize that he was not in the pet shop. He looked around for the puppies that had been in a wire cage next to his aquarium. The puppies were gone. The alligator wondered where the puppies were. Lee Mellon was holding the alligator in his hands.

"Hello, alligator!" Lee Mellon shouted. The alligator was still looking for the puppies. Where had they gone?

"You like frog legs?" Lee Mellon shouted to the alligator and put the alligator carefully down into the pond. The alligator lay there stationary like a toy boat. Lee Mellon gave him a little push and the alligator sailed out into the pond.

There was an instant silence over the pond as if the

pond had been dropped right into the heart of a cemetery. Lee Mellon took the second alligator out of the box.

The second alligator looked all around for the puppies. He couldn't find them either. Where had they gone to?

Lee Mellon stroked the back of the alligator and put it down into the pond and floated it away, and the silence in the pond was multiplied by two. Silence hung like mist over the pond.

"Well, that takes care of the frogs," Elaine whispered finally. We had been hypnotized by the silence.

Lee Mellon stood there staring incredulously at the dark watery silence. "They're gone," he said.

"Yeah," I said. "There's nothing in there now but alligators."

The Rites of Tobacco

NIGHT AND HOW PLEASANT it was to lie there in bed with Elaine curled about me like vines upon my shadow. She had outflanked the locusts of memory and that dismal plague with the equally dismal Cynthia.

The way I felt about it now a salmon could fall on her in Ketchikan. I could see the headline in the Ketchikan newspaper: SALMON FALLS ON GIRL and a nice sub-headline: "Crushed Flatter than a Pancake."

My hand went over Elaine's face and found her mouth. Her lips were parted and I ran my fingers gently along her teeth and touched the sleeping tip of her tongue. I felt like a musician touching a darkened piano.

Before I fell asleep thoughts of Lee Mellon passed again in ordered columns carrying banners and drums down my mind. I thought about a distant and historical time called THREE DAYS BEFORE. I thought about Lee Mellon's Rites of Tobacco.

He had used up all his tobacco and was in desperate

need of a cigarette, so he took the inevitable trip to Gorda. A tobacco jaunt in the sun. It was his fifth or sixth time out since I had been there.

Lee Mellon's Rites of Tobacco went something like this: when he had no more tobacco and no more hope of getting any through the accepted tobacco channels of reality, he would take a hike to Gorda. Of course he had no money to buy any tobacco with, so he would walk along one side of the highway. Say first the side next to the Santa Lucia Mountains, and he would look along the edge of the highway for cigarette butts, and all that he found he would put in a paper bag.

Sometimes he would find a gathering of cigarette butts like a ring of mushrooms in an enchanted forest, but sometimes he would have to walk a mile for a cigarette butt. Then he would flash a six-toothed wonder when he finally found one. In other lands it might be called a smile.

Sometimes after he had walked a half a mile or so and hadn't found a cigarette butt, he would get very depressed and have a fantasy that he would never find another cigarette butt, that he would walk all the way to Seattle without finding one on the highway, and he would turn east and walk all the way to New York, looking carefully month after month along the highway for a cigarette butt without ever finding one. Not a damn one, and the end of an American dream.

It was five miles back to Gorda. Then Lee Mellon would turn around and walk back on the Pacific side of the highway. Down below the Pacific would be throwing its ashes upon the rocks and the shore. Cormorants would be tossing the air with their wings. Whales and pelicans, too, doing each to each the Pacific Ocean.

Like a kind of weird Balboa, Lee Mellon would look for cigarette butts on the shores of the Western World, and the

five miles back to our place, finding here and there an out-
cast of the tobacco kingdom.

When he got back home he would go and sit in front of
the fireplace and take out all the cigarette butts and break
them down until they were a pile of loose tobacco on a
newspaper. Then he would very carefully mix them all together and dividedividedivide the tobacco againagainagain
into itself and put the mixture into an empty tin can.

Lee Mellon's Rites of Tobacco had renewed themselves,
pleasure to be measured like great art, smoke to be counted
like famous paintings hanging in the lungs.

Lee Mellon was the last thing I remembered before I fell
asleep assumed in gentle and loving portions about Elaine.
Lee Mellon fell apart at the edges like tobacco crumbling.

Wilderness Again

I WOKE UP THE NEXT MORNING, sun shining through the glass, but Elaine was not under the sleeping bag with me. I was startled . . . where? Then I saw her bending over the motorcycle parts. She didn't have any clothes on and the sight of her butt renewed my faith in evolution.

"This motorcycle," she said aloud to herself. She sounded like a mother hen admonishing one of her chicks for falling apart.

"This motorcycle," she repeated. *You bad chick! Where's your head!*

"Hello," I said. "You got a nice keester."

She turned toward me and smiled. "I was just looking at this motorcycle. It needs something," she said.

"Yeah, an undertaker," I said. "A motorcycle coffin, a few good words said over it and then a slow majestic final ride out to Marbletown. You have nice breasts," I said.

The sun coming through the window made the room smell like hot motorcycle as if motorcycle were some kind of roast meat.

I'd like a slice of motorcycle on dark rye, please.
Anything to drink sir; gasoline?
No. No, I don't think so.

Elaine put her hands over her breasts. She looked coyish. "Guess who I am?"

"OK, who are you?"

She cocked her head and smiled.

I saw something approaching at the edge of my vision. It was Lee Mellon coming up the path. I waved for him to go back to the hole in the kitchen wall.

He was reluctant to go. He made the motions of eating breakfast, accompanied with facial expressions to show how good the food was. It was quite a breakfast with pork chops and eggs and fried potatoes and fresh fruit.

A rabbit ran behind Lee Mellon. He did not see it and the rabbit hid in the brush and stared out, ears flat against its head. Could Alice be far behind on this beautiful Big Sur morning?

"That's who you are?" I said to Elaine. She nodded her head . . . yes. Breakfast became even more obscure. The hands no longer over the breasts, the body tilted at an angle, slightly forward.

I gave Lee Mellon one HELL-OF-A-WAVE back and he retreated slowly to the hole in the kitchen wall, his inevitable Wilderness.

The Pork Chop Alligator

IT WAS JUST STARTING TO RAIN when we got down to break-fast. Light was tucked like artillery in and out of the clouds, and a warm rain was coming down off the light. Thirty degrees of the sky out over the Pacific was one great army: the Army of the Potomac with General Ulysses S. Grant, Commander in Chief. Lee Mellon was feeding a pork chop to one of the alligators. And Elizabeth was there.

"Nice alligators," she said, smiling with teeth born on the moon and the dark of her nostrils looked carved from jade.

"Have a pork chop," Lee Mellon said, stuffing a pork chop down the alligator's throat. The alligator was sitting on his lap. The alligator said, "GROWL!—opp/opp/opp/opp/opp/opp/opp/opp!" with the end of the pork chop sticking out of his mouth.

Elizabeth had an alligator on her lap. Her alligator didn't say anything. There was no pork chop sticking out of his mouth.

A beautiful gentleness glowed from her as if she had lanterns under her skin. Her beauty made me feel disconsolate.

"Hello," I said.

"Hello, Jesse."

She remembered me.

"This is Elaine," I said.

"Hello, Elaine."

"GROWL!—opp/opp/opp/opp/opp/opp/opp/opp!" the alligator said with the pork chop sticking out of his mouth.

Nothing Elizabeth's alligator said profoundly, for meek alligators shall inherit the earth.

"I'm hungry," I said.

"I'll bet," Lee Mellon said.

Elizabeth was wearing a plain white dress.

"What's for breakfast?" Elaine said.

"A museum," Lee Mellon answered.

"I've never seen any alligators down here before," Elizabeth said. "They're cute. What are they good for?"

"Frog baths," Elaine said.

"Companionship," Lee Mellon said. "I'm lonely. Our alligators could make beautiful music together."

His alligator said, "GROWL!—opp/opp/opp/opp/opp/opp/opp/opp!"

"Your alligator looks like a harp," Elizabeth said, as if she really meant it: with strings coming off her words.

"Your alligator looks like a handbag filled with harmonicas," Lee Mellon said, lying like a dog with dog whistles coming off his words.

"Up your alligator!" I said. "Is there any coffee?"

They both laughed. Elizabeth's voice had a door in it. When you opened that door you found another door, and that door opened yet another door. All the doors were nice and led out of her.

Elaine was looking at me.

"Let's make some coffee," I said.

"There is some coffee," Lee Mellon said. "You didn't hear me."

"I'll get it," Elaine said.

"I'll go with you."

"Good," she said.

That great dark cloud moved up a few degrees, a clock and a rush of wind came by the cabin. The wind made me think about the Battle of Agincourt for it moved like arrows about us, through the very air. Ah, Agincourt: the beauty is all in the saying.

"I'll put another log on the fire," I said. BANG! I hit my head. The coffee turned two white cups inside out, mid-nightly.

"I'll have a cup of coffee if there's enough," Elizabeth said. Make that a third white cup to the black inside out.

"Let's have some breakfast," somebody said. Perhaps it was me. I could very easily have said something like that for I was very hungry.

The pork chops and eggs were good, along with some fried potatoes and that good strawberry jam. Lee Mellon had a second breakfast with us.

He took the pork chop out of the alligator's mouth and used the alligator for a table to rest his plate on. "Fry this one up for me," Lee Mellon said. "It's tenderized now."

The alligator stopped saying, "GROWL!—opp/opp/opp/opp/opp/opp/opp/opp!" Tables should not say things like that.

The Wilderness Alligator Haiku

IT WAS NOW raining very hard and the wind roared like the Confederate army through the hole in the kitchen wall: Wilderness—thousands of soldiers taking up miles of the countryside—Wilderness!

Elizabeth and Lee Mellon had gone off to another cabin. They had to talk about something. Elaine and I were left holding the alligators. We didn't mind.

❦

May 6, 1864. A lieutenant fell to the ground mortally wounded. Collapsing sideways into memory, marble of a classic gender began to grow on his fingerprints. As he lay there sublime in history, another bullet struck his body, causing it to jerk like a shadow in a motion picture. Perhaps Birth of a Nation.

He Usually Stays Over by the Garden

"Ouch!" Elizabeth said. "This ceiling." *The terror of it* and then sat down.

We put the alligators back into the pond. They both sank slowly to the bottom. It was now raining so hard on the pond that you could not see the bottom, nor wanted to.

Elizabeth was sitting there. The white dress was like a swan about her body. As she talked a lake flowed from the swan, answering for eternity that great question: Which came first the lake or the swan?

"I saw the ghost last night," she said. "He was out by the chicken house. I don't know what he was doing there. He usually stays over by the garden. In the corn."

"The ghost?" Elaine said.

"Yes, we have a ghost down here," Elizabeth said. "It's the ghost of an old man. That's his house up there on the plateau. The old man got so old that he had to go and live in Salinas, and they say he died there of a broken heart, and

113

his ghost returned to Big Sur and sometimes he walks around at night. I don't know what he does during the daytime.

"I saw him last night. I don't know what he was doing by the chicken house. I opened the window and said, 'Hello, ghost. What are you doing out by the chicken house? You're usually by the garden. What's wrong?'

"Then the ghost yelled, 'Charge!' waved a large flag and ran into the woods."

"A flag?" Elaine said.

"That's right," Elizabeth said. "He was a veteran of the Spanish-American War."

"Oh. Does he frighten the children?"

"No," Elizabeth said. "They like company. This country is a little lonely for children. Ghosts are welcome. Besides he usually stays over by the garden." Elizabeth was now smiling.

The alligators bobbed to the top of the pond. It stopped raining. Elizabeth was wearing a white dress. Lee Mellon scratched his head. Night came. I said something to Elaine. The pond was quiet like the *Mona Lisa*.

❦

"Where's Private Augustus Mellon?" the captain said.

"I don't know where he is. He was here just a minute ago," the sergeant answered. He had a long yellow mustache.

"He's always here just a minute ago. He's never here now. Probably out stealing something as usual," the captain said.

That Chopping Sound

WE WENT UP TO THE CABIN and to bed. Elizabeth had to do something with Lee Mellon. Her children were in King City, visiting somebody. Elaine took off her clothes. I was very sleepy. I don't remember anything. I just closed my eyes or they closed themselves.

Then there was something moving me. Too nice to be an earthquake, but persistent in its motion, as if the sea had grown small and warm and human and beside me. Then the sea had a voice. "Wake up, wake up, Jesse," Elaine's voice: "Wake up, Jesse. Do you hear that chopping sound?"

"What is it, Elaine?" I said, rubbing the darkness because my eyes were darkness.

"It's a chopping sound, Jesse."

"No, say that again."

"A chopping sound. It's a chopping sound."

"All right," I said and stopped rubbing the darkness. *Let it be a chopping sound. Let it be a beautiful chopping sound,* and I started back down toward sleep.

"Wake up, Jesse!" she said. "It's a chopping sound!"

OK! and I was awake then and it was a chopping sound as if someone were chopping down a forest. Maybe a gang of them. "That's a chopping sound all right," I said. "I guess I'd better go find out what it is."

"That's what I've been trying to tell you," she said.

I lit the lantern: *oh, well, here we go again. The last time led to thee.* "What time is it?" I asked. I rolled over and looked down at Elaine. She looked nice.

"I'm not a clock," she said.

I put my clothes on.

"I'll stay here," Elaine said. "No, I'll go with you."

"It's up to you," I said. "That may be Paul Bunyan out there, desperate for a lay, but it's probably someone trying to steal gasoline with an ax."

"With an ax?"

"Yeah, they do it all the time. Sometimes they steal our gasoline with plows, shoehorns, kangaroo pouches, you know."

"What's so different about your gasoline?" Elaine said.

"It's here," I said.

I slipped a knife into my belt.

"What's that for? What are you trying to do? William-Bonney me?"

"No, no."

"It's up to you," she said. "If you want to go around looking like that."

"There might be a nut or something out there. Besides it's a vaudeville act that Lee Mellon and I perform. I do all the cutting. He does the shooting. Damn good job, too," I said, touching softly her hair: *O gun-gathered lady of my heart!*

The night was cool and the stars were clear like fluid: twinkle, twinkle, little martini star, the same star that led me to thee. Is somebody using an ax to steal our gasoline with?

163 axes full of gasoline.

We'll find out, little star. We have no other choice, being the dominant creature on this shit pile. We have to look after ourselves.

That chopping sound came from the other side of the highway, up along that ragged road. It came loud and unabetted in its hackEty/wackEty: CHOP!

We used the darkness for a light and Elaine held close to me as I found our way along the road like a spoon probing carefully through a blindman's soup, looking for alphabets.

"Why didn't you bring a light?" Elaine said.

"I don't want anybody to know we are here."

"We're not," she said.

We saw a strange light in front of us, coming from the middle of that chopping sound.

"I wonder what it is," Elaine whispered.

"It ain't a time warp," I said, as we approached until we were there and saw a pair of car headlights turned like visionary hooks into the mountain, and a little man with a large ax chopping down trees and piling them on top of his car.

The car looked like a forest now, light coming out as if the moon were somewhere in there or fireworks of it.

"Good morning," I said.

The man stopped and looked at me. He was startled. "Is that you, Amigo Mellon?" he said.

"No," I said.

"Yes, it is," Lee Mellon said and there he was suddenly standing beside us. Elaine jumped like a fish against my arm.

"Good morning, Amigo Mellon," the man said. He looked kind of frenzied standing there with an ax in his hand and a forest stacked on top of his car.

"What are you up to, sport?" Lee Mellon said, now standing in front of me, looking curiously concentrated.

"Covering my car up with trees so they won't find me. They're looking for me. The cops. I'm on the lam. I just paid a two hundred dollar speeding ticket. Can I use this place for a hideout, Amigo Mellon?"

"Sure, just stop chopping down trees."

"Who's that with you? They're not the law, are they? Is that woman a detective?"

"No, this is my buddy and his lady friend."

"Are they married?"

"Yeah."

"Good. I hate the law."

And then he started chopping down another tree. A redwood tree about four feet in diameter. "Hold it, sport," Lee Mellon said.

"What's up, Amigo Mellon?"

"I think you've chopped down enough trees for today."

"I don't want them to find the car."

"You've already got a forest on it," Lee Mellon said. "What kind of car is that, anyway?"

It looked like a sort of sports car all covered with trees, certainly not like the way they do it at the Grand Prix.

"That's my Bentley Bomb, Amigo Mellon."

"Well, I think you've chopped down enough trees. Why don't you turn the lights out. The police won't find you if you keep your lights out."

"Good idea," the man said.

He took some of the trees off the car and got the door of the car open and doused the lights. Then he closed the door and piled the trees back on top of the car.

He picked up a paper bag that was in the brush. Instinctively he knew where it was in the sudden darkness. There seemed to be bottles in the bag.

"Hide me out, Amigo Mellon," he said. The man sort of looked like Humphrey Bogart in *High Sierra*, except that he was short, fat, bald-headed and looked like a guilty businessman because somewhere he had also found a brief-case and had it cemented under his arm.

"Let's go, Roy Earle," Lee Mellon said, touching the same ether that I was touching: the character Humphrey Bogart played in *High Sierra*.

And we walked down from High Sur now, the four of us together, engendered by the fates, Roy Earle and Lee Mellon gradually taking the lead.

❦

A fragment off a cannon ball shattered the branch of a tree and it fell into a spring. The impact of water and branch together was almost like a newspaper headline: WHERE'S AUGUSTUS MELLON? as black mud churned up from the bottom.

A horse lay smoldering in the brush. A great din of rifle fire almost stirred the horse into flames immediate as the year 1864.

A Short History of America
After the War Between the States

ELIZABETH WAS SITTING beside the fireplace when we came down through the hole in the kitchen wall. She did not have her white dress on. She had a gray blanket wrapped around herself like a ragged Confederate uniform. She was staring into the fire. She hardly looked up when we came in.

"Is that a detective?" Roy Earle said, jumping around and shifting the bag. "She looks like a detective. One of those lady-purse-snatching detectives. With a tear gas fountain pen in her purse."

Elizabeth of course had stopped looking into the fire by this time and was staring incredulously at Roy Earle who was really beginning to dance around.

"Who are you?" she asked as if she were addressing a bug.

"I'm Johnston Wade," he said. "I'm head cheese of the Johnston Wade Insurance Company in San Jose. What do you mean who am I? I'm a big shot. I've got a $100,000 in this briefcase, and two bottles of Jim Beam in this sack, and some cheese, too, and a pomegranate."

"This is Roy Earle," Lee Mellon said, introducing the stranger to Elizabeth. "He's crazy and on the lam."

"You don't think this is a $100,000?" Roy Earle said, taking a $100,000 out of the briefcase, and all put together in neat $100 bundles.

And then he dropped down on his knees beside Elizabeth. He looked her hard in the eye and said, "You're passable. I'll give you $3,500 to sleep with me. Cash on the barrel head."

Elizabeth drew the gray uniform closer about her shoulders. She looked away into the fire. A log was burning there, but there were no bugs staring out at her, no bon voyage, no have a nice trip.

"We don't want to hear any of that," Lee Mellon said like the gallant Confederate general he was.

Roy Earle looked at Elaine. Frenzy dripped off him like a flood of detergent soapsuds roaring through the Carlsbad Caverns. "I'll give you $2,000," he said.

"Get rid of him," I said.

"I'll handle this, Jesse. I know this bird." Lee Mellon turned and looked very concentrated at Roy Earle. "Shut up, sport," he said. "Sit down over there and keep your lips flat on your face."

Roy Earle went over and sat down against the wooden wall. He put the $100,000 back into the briefcase. He put the briefcase on the floor and then he put his feet on the briefcase. He sat there with his feet on his briefcase and took a bottle of Jim Beam out of the paper bag.

He broke the seal on the bottle, unscrewed the cap and poured a big slug of whiskey into his mouth. He swallowed it down with a hairy gulp. Strange, for as I said before: he was bald.

He went UMMM-good, smacked his lips and rolled his eyes like the octopus ride in a cheap carnival. He put the bottle back into the paper bag, and then looked innocent as a newborn baby.

That made Lee Mellon mad.

"Hold it, sport."

"What's up, Amigo Mellon?"

"The sauce is up, sport."

"The sauce?"

"Yeah, the King James Version of the Bible you got there in that sack, sport."

"Oh, you want a drink?"

"I don't want a lifesaver."

"That's very funny." Roy Earle started laughing like hell and took his feet off his money, rolled back onto the floor and began kicking his feet in the air like mashed potatoes. Then he sat back up and put his feet down on his money.

He stared straight ahead at us, and suddenly it was as if he were not there at all. He was just sitting there smiling, but it was terrible. False teeth showed in a light that dangled like an illuminated grave off them. He really looked in bad shape, hardly human any more.

Lee Mellon looked at him, shook his head slowly, walked over and took the paper bag out of his hand, opened it up, removed the bottle of Jim Beam, took a big slug of it, handed it to Elizabeth, who did likewise, wrapped in the Confederate uniform.

Elizabeth handed it to me. I handed it to Elaine. She took a medium slug out of it, and handed it back.

BANG! I hit my God-damn head on the ceiling and

took some of the whiskey to stop the pain. It did. With
Roy Earle smiling all the time.

"Let's go have a talk, Roy," Lee Mellon said.

"My name is Johnston Wade. I run the Johnston Wade
Insurance Company in San Jose. My wife wants to put me
in the nuthouse because I bought a new car: my Bentley
Bomb. She wants all my money and so does my son who
goes to Stanford and my daughter who goes to Mills College.

"They want to lock Pop up, put Pop away in the
nuthouse. Well, I got a surprise for them. I just paid a
$200 speeding ticket and they can all go to hell.

"What do you think about that, huh? Pop's too smart
for them. I went down to the bank and I got all the money
and the stocks and bonds and deeds and jewelry, and I got
a pomegranate, too."

He reached into the bag and took out the pomegranate.
He held it up as if he were a magician showing off the end
product of a trick.

"I bought it in Watsonville," he said. "For a dime. The
best dime I ever spent in my life. That cunt in Mills College
learning arithmetic and modern dance and how to screw her
dear old dad out of everything he earned, she won't get that
dime.

"That asshole son at Stanford, learning to be a doctor,
he won't get that dime out of his dear old pop's gullet. Ha-ha.

"That bridge-playing psychopath, my wife, who's trying to lock me up because I want a Bentley Bomb. That
pomegranate dime's gone. She won't spend that dime on her
lover in Morgan Hill.

"I run the Johnston Wade Insurance Company in San
Jose. I am Johnston Wade. Just because I'm fifty-three years
old and want a sports car, they think they're going to lock
me up, put me away. They got another think coming. Fuck
'em.

"My lawyer told me to get every cent I got and run for cover, go on the lam. They won't find me down here. Will they, Amigo Mellon?

"My lawyer's going to send me a telegram down at my hidden hunting lodge in San Diego. Near where I got my moose and my Kodiak bear.

"He's going to send me a telegram when everything is all clear, when he's put the kibosh on their plans. That's right. Ain't it, Amigo Mellon?"

Then he was instantly quiet. He stared at us with that same stupid smile on his face. He said all these things to us as if he were a prisoner of war, giving his name, rank and serial number.

❦

A crow had somehow grown webs about itself, driven by the fear of the Wilderness. Other creatures: mice, beetles, rabbits had also grown webs about themselves, usurping the spiders that were now long and slender and like worms in the ground, waiting for the entrance of graves.

A boy of sixteen, uniform torn awry like a playground in an earthquake, lay dead next to an old man of fifty-nine, uniform solemn as a church, complete, closed, dead.

Lee Mellon's San Jose Sartorious

WE WERE STUNNED. Lee Mellon led him away. He was totally shattered. Nobody said anything. We couldn't and the stars were silent out over the sea. They had to be.

Elizabeth went back to staring into the fire. Elaine sat down. We waited for Lee Mellon. The stars waited. Elizabeth waited. Elaine waited. I, and even waiting itself waited, second only to the stars because they had been at it a longer time.

"HURRAY FOR AMIGO MELLON!" Roy Earle yelled from the next cabin down.

"SHUT UP, YOU NUT!"

"HURRAY FOR AMIGO MELLON!"

"NUT! NUT!"

Then silence again, the stars out over us . . . Elizabeth silence. "Coffee?" Elaine said, trying to make reality out of what we had to deal with. It made me think of a French cook trying to work with a two-headed dragon onion.

"That would be good," I said, trying to help out a little

for I wanted reality to be there. What we had wasn't worth it. Reality would be better.

Elaine made some coffee. It didn't help at all.

I had a vision of Lee Mellon as the world's only Confederate psychiatrist: Zurich-trained, battleflag-draped, Maryland!-My-Maryland! psychiatrist into Big Sur, into dreams, and this reality into here.

Elizabeth was staring into the fire, and Elaine's coffee had become a nervous trait. She fidgeted with it.

"YOU NUT!" Amigo Mellon's voice cut through the darkness. Yes, psychiatry in action, another mind being led to the path of light by our gallant laurel-crowned, laurel-gathered psychiatrist.

"He seems to be having trouble," Elizabeth said.

The stars didn't say anything. They waited. My cup of coffee changed into an albino polar bear: I mean, cold and black. I threw it into the pond.

Then Lee Mellon appeared. He looked tired. He had the whiskey with him, a bottle in each hand. He offered us all a drink, spreading the whiskey about like martial music. "You might as well leave him with a loaded gun," Lee Mellon said. "The guy's out of it. The only way you can treat him is like a nut. He responds to it because he is a nut."

"He's pretty far out," I said.

"Yes," the women said.

The whiskey went well. I wish I could have offered the stars a drink. Looking down upon mortals, they probably need a drink from time to time, certainly on a night like this. We got drunk.

"Who is he?" I said.

"He came down here six months ago," Lee Mellon said. "He had the same story. Stayed three days. Crazy as a rattlesnake in dog days, a real dingo. He took me up to his

place in San Jose. On the way we honky-tonked at Nepenthe
for a couple of days. He spent $2,000 and we went up to his
place in San Jose.

"His family shit when they saw me. They're just like
he described them. Bad news.

"He was going to give me a truck he had in the garage.
His layout was really something: three stories high, lots
of lawns and flowers around. A jap gardener. You know,
up in those fancy hills back of San Jose where the big
money subdivides.

"I stayed with him for a month. God, did that cunt
family of his have no use for me. And all I wanted was
the fucking truck.

"I stayed around his place drinking that good wine he
bought by the case, and listening to records on his hi-fi. He
took me around to all the fancy San Jose eats. Wined and
dined me, he did. He didn't come on with me at all, didn't
put the make on me.

"I must have drunk ten cases of the good stuff. I
bugged the shit out of his family. The hi-fi had about a
hundred speakers. I turned the hi-fi up so loud that I
reduced that house to tears. And all I wanted was the God-
damn fucking truck.

"Roy put a couple thousand dollars worth of fancy
camping equipment and wine and canned lobster and shit in
the truck. He gave me everything but the fucking keys.

"I used to go out to the garage all the time and look
at the truck. God, it sure looked purty. The guy was
completely out of his mind. Just nutty. Almost as bad as he
is now. The only way you can treat him is just like a nut,
tell him to shut up, sit down, when to pee, etc.

"It really bugged the daughter when I yelled, 'SHUT
UP, YOU NUT!' to her father. One morning I was lying in
a puddle of wine when suddenly I was awakened by the wife.

And she said, 'It's time to leave now. I've already called the police. You've got about sixty seconds to be on your way, you sponge.'

"I took a quick look around for Roy. He was of course gone. I think they had him under observation, so I had to light out: no truck, nothing.

"I was so drunkied up that I even forgot my shoes. I arrived back here with no shoes. Hard as hell hitch-hiking, too. Finally got a ride on the back of a fertilizer truck, sitting on the shit.

"I haven't heard from him since. Thought they had him locked up. He's in a lockup way, but he really is a big shot. Still smart, too.

"While I was down there at the other cabin he slipped away and buried that briefcase full of money some place. He came back covered all over with dirt, looked like he was waylayed and raped by a gravedigger."

❧

WHERE's AUGUSTUS MELLON? on the front page of the Wilderness Bugle. *Turn to page 17 for Robert E. Lee. Turn to page 100 for an interesting story about alligators.*

The Camp-fires of Big Sur

I see before me now a traveling army halting,
Below a fertile valley spread, with barns and the
*   orchards of summer,*
Behind, the terraced sides of a mountain, abrupt,
*   in places rising high,*
Broken, with rocks, with clinging cedars, with tall
*   shapes dingily seen,*
The numerous camp-fires scatter'd near and far,
*   some away up on the mountain,*
The shadowy forms of men and horses, looming,
*   large-sized, flickering,*
And over all the sky—the sky! far, far out of
*   reach, studded, breaking out, the eternal stars.*
                                    —WHITMAN

WE KILLED THE WHISKEY in that hour before dawn. It lay
like the prophecy of a battle at our feet. The stars did late
things in the sky and were fastened by picture wire above
our future. Then we saw a fire just a ways down the coast,

perhaps three or four hundred yards. The fire loomed up and grew in momentum and speed and importance.

Lee Mellon took out running and I was running after him, stumbling. We got there just in time for the fire was only a moment away from being out of control.

While we were putting out the fire, beating and whacking and clawing at the flames with dirt and branches, throwing fire on fire to put out fire, Roy Earle was saying, "Ha-ha fire."

I thought Lee Mellon was going to slug him, but all Lee Mellon did was sit him down and tell him to cover his eyes with his hands, and he did so, but he kept saying, "Ha-ha fire." And then there wasn't any fire.

"I hope they didn't see that down at the lighthouse," Lee Mellon said. "It's twenty-five miles away, but they see real good, and I don't want them to come up here and poke around. It wouldn't make sense."

We were both smoky and sweating and blackened and inflamed with exhaustion. We didn't look very good, like an advanced case of Smokey Bear leukemia.

Roy Earle sat there cool as a cucumber with his hands over his eyes: See no evil, hear no evil, speak no evil, except for ha-ha fire, and above all, suddenly, the great transcendental fire department of American history, Walt Whitman, fire chief, with the stars like fire engines hanging in the air and streams of light coming from their hoses.

Private Augustus Mellon thirty-seven-year-old former slave trader in residence at a famous Southern university ran for his life among the casual but chess-like deaths in the Wilderness. Fear gripped every stitch of his clothing and would have gripped his boots if he'd had a pair.

He ran barefooted through a spring with a shattered branch lying in it, and he saw a horse smoldering in the brush, and a crow covered with spider webs, and two dead soldiers lying next to each other, and he could almost hear his own name, Augustus Mellon, searching for himself.

The Discovery of Laurel

WE ALL WENT TO BED AFTER THAT. Elaine and I to the glass house. There were some quail at the edge of the garden and they flew away back up the mountain.

Lee Mellon did something with Roy Earle. I don't know what he did, but he said that Roy Earle wouldn't start any more fires while they got some sleep: the Confederate general and his lady.

"I'm very tired," Elaine said as we lay down.

"You know something?" I said.

"No, what?"

"The next time you hear a chopping sound, do me a favor and forget about it."

"All right," and we cradled together. It grew cloudy again and we were able to sleep without the hot sun coming in through the window.

We woke up in the middle of the afternoon. "I want to be layed," Elaine said.

All right. I layed her but my mind was elsewhere. I don't know where it was at.

When we got down to the cabin Elizabeth was there. She looked beautiful. "Good morning," she said.

"Hi, and good morning," we said.

"Where's Lee?" I said.

"He's gone to get Roy."

"Where's Roy at?"

"I don't know. Lee put him some place."

"I wonder where he put him?" Elaine said.

"I don't know but Lee said he wouldn't start any more fires. Roy had obviously been there before because he said, 'I don't want to go.' But Lee told him it wouldn't be as bad this time as it was before. Lee said he could have a blanket. Does this make any sense?" Elizabeth said.

"I wonder where that is?" I said. "There aren't too many places you can put somebody down here."

"I don't know," she said. "But here they come."

Lee Mellon and Roy Earle were talking as they came up the path from the lower cabin.

"You were right, Amigo Mellon," Roy Earle said. "It wasn't as bad this time as it was before. That blanket really helped out."

"I told you so, didn't I?" Lee Mellon said.

"Yeah, but I didn't believe it."

"You've got to have more faith," Lee Mellon said.

"It's pretty hard to have faith when everybody is trying to lock you up," Roy Earle said.

Then they were with us.

"Good morning," Roy Earle said cheerfully. He was acting as if his muscles were a little cramped, but he seemed to be in a lot better mental shape.

"Howdy," Lee Mellon said. He went over and kissed

Elizabeth on the mouth. They put their arms around each other.

I looked down at the alligators in the pond. 75 per cent of their eyes were staring back at me.

We had breakfast.

Roy Earle ate a great big breakfast along with us and then he began to go insane again. Food seemed to abet his madness.

"Nobody's going to find my money," Roy Earle said. "I buried it."

"Fuck your money," somebody said: me.

Roy began rooting around the rocks in the fireplace and he found something stuffed behind one of the rocks. It was wrapped in plastic.

Roy unwrapped it, looked at it very carefully, smelled it and then said, "This looks like marijuana."

Lee Mellon walked over. "Let me look at that." He took a look at it. "It's oregano," he told Roy Earle.

"Looks like marijuana to me."

"It's oregano."

"I'll bet you a $1,000 it's dope," Roy Earle said.

"No, it's oregano. Very good in spaghetti," Lee Mellon said. "I'll put it in the kitchen. The next time we make spaghetti we can use it."

Lee Mellon went and put the dope in the kitchen. Roy Earle shrugged his shoulders. The rest of the day passed quietly. Elizabeth looked beautiful. Elaine was nervous. Roy Earle got deeply involved in watching the alligators.

He looked at them and smiled and was quietly amused for the rest of the day until about sundown. SUDDENLY he stared at the pond and said in a voice filled with earthquakes, pestilence and apocalypse, "MY GOD, THEY ARE ALLIGATORS!"

Lee Mellon led him away. He was totally shattered.

"They are alligators. They are alligators. They are alligators," he kept saying over and over again until we could not hear his voice any more.

Lee Mellon took him and put him away where he kept him. I don't know where that could have been. I don't even want to think about it: a Confederate flag over Zurich.

❧

He saw some Union soldiers coming through a thicket. He dove forward onto the ground and pretended that he was dead, though it would not have made any difference if he had been dead and pretended to be alive. The Union soldiers were so scared that they did not see him. None of them had guns, anyway. They had thrown their guns away and were looking for a Confederate to surrender to. Of course Augustus Mellon did not know this, lying there as he was, eyes pretending to be closed forever, breath silenced for all time.

Lee Mellon, Roll Away! You Rolling River

LEE MELLON CAME BACK without Roy Earle. "He's cosy as a bug in a rug."

"Where are you putting him?" I said.

"Don't worry about it. He's OK and has a lovely view of the ocean. After all he's a nut. We can't let him run around and turn Big Sur into a torch. He's OK. Don't worry."

"Analytical psychology à la Jung, huh?" I said.

"Don't be so funny," Lee Mellon said. "He's OK. I'm taking good care of him."

"All right," I said. "You're in residence here."

"Then do I have your permission to go and get the dope?" Lee Mellon said. "I don't know about you but I feel like turning on. Getting a little dopey. OK?"

"Yeah, that sounds OK."

Lee Mellon went into the kitchen and got the dope out of where we kept the spices.

"That's really marijuana that Roy found there in the fireplace?" Elaine whispered to me.

"Yeah," I said.

"Lee Mellon's pretty fast, isn't he?"

"Yeah, I guess he is. Have you ever turned on?"

"No," she said.

"Ah, dope," Lee Mellon said, coming out of the kitchen, carrying the little plastic package in his hand.

"Ah, dreaded narcotics. The evil root. The bad-bad," he said. "I was church people until I discovered this shit. Let's turn on."

"I've never turned on before," Elaine said. "What's it like?"

"Hurry! Hurry!" Lee Mellon said, coming on like a carnival barker. "Dope tours! Dope tours! Get your fresh dope tours! Read all about it! World-renowned eighty-nine-year-old philosopher arrested in jazz musician dope den! Said he thought it was tuna fish! Read all about it! Tangier! Tangier! Albania!"

Elaine was breaking up. Elizabeth was smiling. I was casually memorizing everything and Lee Mellon got a piece of newspaper and put the dope on it, and began to manicure it: to separate the stems and seeds and work the dope up until it was delicate in nature.

"Ah, dope," Lee Mellon kept repeating over and over again. "It's dope. It's dope. Mamma warned me against it. My minister said it would rot the bones in my brain cells. My papa put me over his knee and said, 'Stop turning the barnyard stock on, son. One of the cows laid an egg this morning and one of the rabbits tried to put a saddle on.' Ah, dope. It's dope."

I had never turned on with Lee Mellon before and it looked as if it would be different. The young dope fiend seemed to know what he was up to.

He rolled a surgical joint, lit it up and gave it to his young Confederate lady who inhaled deeply and passed it on to Elaine. She didn't know quite what to do with it.

"Breathe it into your lungs," I said. "And hold it down as long as you can."

"All right," she said.

She did what I told her. Good girl and passed the joint to me. I stoked my lungs with the dope smoke and passed it back to Lee Mellon, and it went around and around and around and around and around until we were there: higher than kites.

Lee Mellon started laughing after about the fifth joint and he continued laughing and he didn't say anything.

"This is pretty good," Elaine said. "But I certainly don't feel any different. Not like a revolution." All the time she said this to me, she was just staring at the fire.

Elizabeth acted like an infinite swan. I mean, that quality advanced beyond the limits of her body and hovered there in the room. "I feel good," she said.

Lee Mellon was just laughing away like hell, then he took all the roach-ends of the dreaded dope sticks and he began to break them down and he ate each piece of charred paper very carefully until they were gone, and then like shuffling a deck of cards he took the little survivors of those dope sticks and rolled them all together into a B-17 bomber, and he lit that one up, like antiaircraft fire over Berlin and sent everybody higher.

Elaine took up permanently staring at the fire. Elizabeth played with her hair while she watched Lee Mellon, who was still laughing away like hell.

He did not seem to have the power of speech any more, so I began pacing back and forth and saying things like, "Hummm, hummm, you seem to have lost the power of speech," and Lee Mellon would laugh even harder than ever.

"Can't talk, huh?"

Lee Mellon shook his head no.

"Can you hear?"

Lee Mellon held up two fingers.

"Good," I said. "The power of speech is obviously gone, but the man can still hear. That's good."

Lee Mellon flashed the two fingers like bombs falling on a city.

"Good. Good. Communication," I said. "That good old yes or no. Contact with the land of the living. You may not be able to speak, to carry on a healthy conversation about politics, but you can flash those two fingers yes and shake that head no. Let's try that again. Flash those fingers for yes, and shake that head for no."

He did it laughing like seven hyenas turned inside out and covered with chicken feathers.

"Yes. Yes, that looks good. After careful examination I say this man is under the influence of narcotics."

Lee Mellon flashed two fingers like Winston Churchill's V for victory.

"Yes, yes, this man reminds me of David Copperfield and those sordid adventures of Mr. Dick and his erotic, neurotic, bubonic kites.

"This man is obviously a fly-by-nighter. Probably never pays his rent, steals goofy shoes, paints the town, has a pair of stuffed seal flippers in his suitcase.

"Yes, this man is definitely under the influence of narcotics. Probably has a Thomas De Quincey costume in his suitcase, along with those stuffed seal flippers."

Lee Mellon beat his hands on the floor like a seal and began making seal sounds. To think that less than an hour before he had been taking care of Roy Earle, and now he needed a keeper himself.

Elizabeth was very amused by the whole scene but she didn't say anything except, "Lee's pretty high."

Elaine was hung up on the fire. She didn't take her eyes off the fire. It was as if for the first time in her life she was seeing fire. It was the fire for her.

"Come off it, Mellon," I said. "Jack London threw that plot away as being too corny. Let's have something a little more original."

Lee Mellon continued to beat his hands on the floor like a seal. Obviously he thought the plot was pretty good. Then I got hung up on Elizabeth's hair. It almost began to move in the light. I was pretty far out myself. Like a marriage.

"Dope's all right," Elaine said finally.

Lee Mellon held up two fingers and Elizabeth's hair affirmed it.

❦

After the Union soldiers had fled in panic, Augustus Mellon waited a while before trying out life again. An ant crawled across his hand. The ant moved as if it had a passport to rheumatism. Augustus Mellon rang forth a tintinnabulation of silent curses, being dead was one thing, this was another.

Alligators Minus Pork Chops

AFTER ABOUT TWO HOURS of speechless laughter Lee Mellon got up and jumped into the pond, and began splashing alligators out of the dark water.

"GROWL!—opp/opp/opp/opp/opp/opp/opp/opp!" They appeared and disappeared from his hands like a sloppy reptile magician performing incoherent alligator tricks.

It took him about fifteen minutes before he caught one of them. He still could not talk and was laughing all the time. What a vision!

Then he made a grand Confederate general gesture and gave the alligator to Elizabeth. She accepted the alligator with a twinkling solemnness. She returned a kiss for it. It was all very touching.

Lee Mellon jumped back into the pond, fell is a better word, I guess. He fell face first into the pond, making a great splash.

At that precise instant Roy Earle appeared at the edge

of the firelight. He was chained to a log he had dragged from God knows where. It was just horrible.

"What's Amigo Mellon up to?" he said, asking a question about his Confederate psychiatrist who was splashing to the surface, laughter coming out of the water.

"Alligators," I said.

"OH, GOD, NO! NO! NO!" Roy Earle screamed, picking up his log and dragging it away into the night. He had appeared as a specter and disappeared as a specter. There was nothing of us in his coming and going. He was just another specter, chained to a log, fleeing alligators at Big Sur.

Lee Mellon came up out of the water with an alligator fastened by its teeth to the collar of his shirt. Lee Mellon stalked out of the water and back into the room, the alligator hanging like a medallion from his neck.

❦

He came upon a Union captain lying headless among the flowers. With no eyes and no mouth, only flowers on top of the neck, the captain looked like a vase. But this did not distract Augustus Mellon to the point of not seeing the captain's boots. Though the captain's head was absent from this world, his boots were not, and they entertained the barefoot fantasies of Augustus Mellon's feet, and then replaced those fantasies with leather. Private Augustus Mellon left the captain even more deficient, even more unable to cope with reality.

Four Couples: An American Sequence

BEFORE WE WENT TO BED, Elaine got so she really liked dope. I don't know what happened to Elizabeth. She went away with Lee Mellon.

They had the alligators with them. I don't know if Lee Mellon was talking or not. Elizabeth said she could drive.

I looked around for Roy Earle. I didn't want him to get up on the highway, chained to that log. It might attract the wrong attention. I do not know what the right attention would be in a case like that. Everything was very strange.

Roy Earle where are you at? I looked all around, carrying a lantern. I left Elaine sitting in front of the fire. She was really hung up on it. She said there was something of all of us in the fire, and I said yeah, and take care of yourself.

"Roy Earle? Roy-baby? Roy?" I looked all around and everywhere and worked my way down to the last cabin. "Roy, everything is all right. The alligators are gone.

Everything's OK. You can come out now. Johnston Wade? Mr. Wade? Wade Insurance Company?"

"In here," a rather calm voice said. "The Wade Insurance Company is in here. In the cabin." It did not sound like Roy Earle, but who else could it be?

I opened the cabin door and brought the lantern in, and there was Mr. Johnston Wade in a double sleeping bag. There was somebody else in the bag with him. For a second I thought that it was Elizabeth, but of course it wasn't, couldn't be. Why should I think that?

"Who's that with you?" I said.

"That's the log," Johnston Wade said. "I couldn't get it off, so I put it in the sack with me."

"Are you all right?" I said.

"Yeah," he said. "But I'm crazy most of the time. I don't know what I'm saying or where I'm at. Where am I and who are you?"

"At Big Sur. I'm Jesse."

"Hello, Jesse."

I turned the lantern away from him and there was a moment of silence after that, and then he said out of the silence, "Just as well. Please go away. I'm very tired."

"Want me to help you get that chain off?" I said.

"No," he said. "It's all right. Actually, I kind of like it. Reminds me of my wife. Good night."

"Good night," I said. I went back and rescued Elaine from the fire. I felt like some weird kind of Saint Bernard dog saving a skier lost in fire.

"It really looks pretty," she said. "You know that we are all in there."

"Yeah," I said. "Let's go to bed."

We passed through the hole in the kitchen wall, effortlessly.

"Where are Lee and Elizabeth?" she said.

"They've gone some place in her car. They took the alligators with them. I don't know where they've gone."

"I saw them in the fire," she said.

❦

Private Augustus Mellon was up and moving. All around him were the sounds of war as if placed under a magnifying glass. Then in the midst of the great rifle fusilade, he heard the unlimbering of artillery like new muscles being used in the Wilderness.

Awaken to the Drums!

I DON'T KNOW HOW LONG we were asleep—I had a dream about Alfred Hitchcock; he said the Civil War was all right —before Elaine began stirring me again: *Oh, no*.

I would not fight it this time. There was no reason ever to fight it again. I opened my eyes. It was early in the morning, and the morning seemed as strange to me as any of the recent events. It was cloudy and cool and the air seemed dead through the glass.

"What's up?" I said.

"Drums," she said. Her voice was tired. "Hear them?"

Yup, I heard them. Drums. They were drums all right, not as violent as Walt Whitman's drums but they certainly were there.

Perhaps the Confederate army was getting ready to move, a new invasion of the North. Who knows? I didn't. Drums.

"Stay here."

I got dressed and went out to see what was up. I

expected to see thousands of ragged Confederate troops going by on Highway 1, with cavalry dashing through and scattering the ranks, and hundreds of wagons filled with ammunition and supplies, and artillery going by, their horses moving at a good pace.

I expected to see a Confederate invasion of Monterey, California, drums and banners going by on Highway 1, but all I saw was Roy Earle, free of his wife, sitting by the hole in the kitchen wall, beating on an overturned washtub.

"What's up?" I said.

"Nothing. I was just trying to drum somebody up," he said rather sanely. "I didn't know where everybody had gone to."

"You did," I said.

❦

Augustus Mellon stumbled into a clearing that had a de luxe muscle building course of artillery at one end of it, and then a furious assault by Texas troops, Hood's old boys against the Union army, and General Robert E. Lee tried to get into it, but those Texans wouldn't allow it, and then the 8th Big Sur Volunteer Heavy Root Eaters arrived and one of them offered Traveller a limpet to eat, and Private Augustus Mellon had a new pair of boots, and then the 8th Big Sur Volunteer Heavy Root Eaters began dancing in a circle, the general and his horse in the middle, while all around them waged the American Civil War, the last good time this country ever had.

Bye Now, Roy Earle,
Take Care of Yourself

ROY EARLE was in fairly good shape when Lee Mellon and Elizabeth drove up in her car. "That's Lee Mellon," Roy Earle said. "That's my amigo, Amigo Mellon."

"Yeah," I said. "Amigo Mellon."

"How did he get loose?" Lee Mellon said, speech having been restored to his mouth like birds to the sky.

"I don't know," I said. "Why did you chain him to a log? Couldn't you have done something else, Dr. Jung?"

"I know how to take care of him," Lee Mellon said.

"Yeah," I said. "Sure, he was running around here last night with a log chained to him. Didn't you see him last night when you were playing Hamlet?"

"Don't worry about it," Lee Mellon said. "Everything's under control now."

"I guess it's all right," I said, feeling a sudden wave

of vacancy go over me, like a hotel being abandoned by its guests for an obvious reason.

While breakfast moved along, Roy Earle was strangely quiet and his features calculated themselves and before breakfast was over, he looked and acted again as he did last night when I went down to the cabin and found him asleep with a log, covered by a green sleeping bag, like a man sticking out of a meadow.

When we finished breakfast, he said, "It's time for me to go now. This is Wednesday, isn't it?"

"Yes, it is," Elizabeth said.

"I have to meet a client in Compton," he said. "I guess I'll be going shortly. It's been very nice meeting you people. You must come up and visit me sometime in San Jose."

"Yes," Lee Mellon said.

Mr. Johnston Wade looked perfectly sane, except of course for his clothes and body that were rather disheveled with Big Sur grime.

"Yes, I have an appointment and must be going now."

"Are you all right?" Elaine said.

"Yes, I am, young lady," he said. "I guess my car's up on that road by those trees."

"Do you have your money?" Elaine said, casting an inquisitional glance toward Lee Mellon: notorious for thought and deed.

"I have my briefcase," Mr. Johnston Wade said and went over and lifted up that horrible deer rug that looked like a toupee for Frankenstein. "Here it is," he said. "I got it this morning."

"Good," I said.

Lee Mellon stared at the pond. It was different without frogs or alligators. I was going to ask Lee Mellon where the alligators were, but I figured it would be better to save that question until Mr. Johnston Wade was on his way to his insurance appointment in Compton.

He took the trees off his car and we said good-bye to him. "Do visit me in San Jose," he yelled out the window as he backed the sports car down the road.

"Yes," Lee Mellon said.

Bon voyage, Roy. Have a nice trip. Bye now, Roy Earle, take care of yourself, but I didn't feel very good at all. More rooms were being vacated. The elevator was jammed with suitcases.

Crowned with Laurel and Our
Banners Before Us We Descend!

WE WENT BACK DOWN to the cabin. The sun came out and a nice sweet smell rose like small invisible birds from the sagebrush and circled about us in the air and followed us down, with a great light on the ocean.

"Well, that takes care of Roy Earle," Lee Mellon said. "You must stop at San Jose and visit him sometime, but I'd bring an extra pair of shoes with you and a getaway car. It's a lot of fun while it lasts.

"I recommend the hi-fi wine. Speaking of hi-fi wine: Let's go down to the Pacific and turn on and go with the waves. They're great on dope.

"I like the way they crack like eggs against the Grand Grill of North America. You like that, huh? You're supposed to be literary."

"Ah, fuck it. Where are the alligators?" I said.

"I'd like to turn on," Elaine said.

"Down at Hearstville," Lee Mellon said.

"Hearseville?"

"No, Hearstville. San Simeon."

"Oh, God, what are they doing down there?"

"We threw them in the pond. You know, Citizen-Kane chess. It seemed like the thing to do," Lee Mellon said. "The frogs are gone. They'll never come back.

"They've probably committed themselves to some place like Norwalk. They're all in psycho-fucking-alligator shock. Bad medicine.

"We thought the alligators should live out the rest of their days peacefully in swell digs. In tune with the Greek temples and the good life. Not like social security."

"All right," I said. "Sounds reasonable."

I was really gone. My mind was beginning to take a vacation from my senses. I felt it continuing to go while Lee Mellon got the dope.

Elizabeth was as usual. Somewhere she had gotten a scarlet sash and Lee Mellon tied it around her waist. We started down the steep rocky path to the Pacific. It looked like a Confererate flag tied about her.

We were strung out behind her like fish in a net. Three whales came by, spouting high and clear. I looked from Elizabeth's waist to the whales. I expected Confederate flags to be flying from their spouts.

To a Pomegranate Ending,
Then 186,000 Endings Per Second

THE PACIFIC OCEAN rolled to its inevitable course: our bodies at the edge with Lee Mellon rolling dope. He handed some to Elaine. She really went at it, and then she handed it to me. I gave it to Elizabeth, who was like a Greek dance, forgotten in Modern Times.

We smoked five or six chunks of dope and then the ocean began to come in on us in a different manner: I mean, slow and light itself.

I looked over at Elizabeth. She was sitting on a white rock, the wind lighting the end of her red banner. She stared out at the ocean with her head in her hands. Lee Mellon was lying flat on his back, sprawled flung out on the rough sand.

Elaine stared at the waves that were breaking like ice cube trays out of a monk's tooth or something like that. Who knows? I don't know.

I was staring at the three of them, high on their earthly presence and my relationship to the presence. I felt very strange and confused inside.

The last week's activities had been a little too much for me, I think. A little bit too much of life had been thrown at me, and I couldn't put it all together. I stared at Elizabeth.

She was beautiful and seagulls flew over the ocean, fastened by harp strings to the surface, Bach and Mozart broke on the foam. We sat there. Four people poleaxed by dope.

Elizabeth was beautiful and the wind got in her hair and lifted up the hem of her white dress and the Confederate banner was curling in its red hair. Elaine sat there alone.

Then she came over to me and said, "Let's take a walk."

"All right," I said. That was my voice, wasn't it? Yes, it was. We walked down a ways, maybe fifty years, and Elaine suddenly put her arms about me and kissed me very hard on the mouth and she put her hand between my legs.

There was nothing girlish about the gesture. She meant it. My, how she had come along. "I want," she said, like a child.

She put her mouth inside my mouth, but I felt very strange. It had been such a long hard week. I felt things slipping in my mind.

"I'll undress you," Elaine said.

I sat down on a place where there was rough sand and small white pebbles and many flies in the air. The flies kept landing on me and Elaine took off my shoes, and then she took off my pants and she noticed that I didn't have an erection.

"We'll get something down there," she said. "Right away." She took off my shorts. I must have put them on when I woke up, but I didn't remember doing so. It really wasn't very important, but it surprised me. Things like that should not surprise a person.

"Off with your shirt," she said. "Now look at you. You don't have any clothes on." She was very pleased with herself, but she seemed awfully strange to me, almost as if she were somebody else.

I wondered what Elizabeth was doing, and things were slipping in my mind. I slapped at a fly on my leg. The flies came from a lot of kelp that had been thrown up on the beach after the storm. Was it really just a couple days before? Must have been.

"I still have my clothes on," Elaine said, and kicked off her shoes. She was really on an erotic thing. I could only look at it like somebody watches a pinball machine.

She took off her shirt and the ocean blew against her and the surf cracked behind her like white marble castles against glasses of Rhine wine.

She was exploiting the maximum amount of drama out of taking off her clothes. It made me think of *Hamlet,* some kind of weird *Hamlet* where maybe Ophelia would take her clothes off like Elaine was doing.

Her breasts tensed up at the shock of the cold. Her nipples hardened like stones in the mind. The surface of her skin acted cinematographically to the cold.

She was wearing a pair of jeans. Strange, I hadn't noticed that all day. She pulled them down slowly, floated them down her hips like statues coming down a river on rafts.

Why would anyone want to do something like that? I didn't have an erection.

I didn't feel any desire. I looked between my legs and there were small white pebbles, just a little bit larger than sand. I looked at them and a fly landed on my shoulder. I shrugged him off.

Elaine stopped her jeans right in the middle of her vagina. It looked strange to me. I didn't know what to think about it.

I couldn't get an erection. Maybe it would come later. Strange, maybe she could help me out with it. I didn't feel very good.

Of course she would help me out. This was just a little thing.

She stepped out of her jeans and moved toward me like a rhythm. She got down on her knees in front of me. I looked at the white rocks under my penis and the shadow of her head came over the top of them and put them entirely in the shade.

But nothing worked and the flies crawled on us. I got on top of her, hoping that might do it, but the flies crawled all over us and nothing happened. Nothing happened for a long time.

Who said we were the dominant creature on this shit pile? The flies were teaching an advanced seminar in philosophy as they crawled up the crack of my ass.

After a while it was apparent to everybody: Elaine the sky, Elaine the Pacific Ocean, Elaine the sand, Elaine the sun, Elaine, Elaine, Elaine . . .

"It's all right," she said. "It's all right." That was really a very nice sound. There should be a bird that does that: that sings when you are impotent.

"You poor dear," she said. "You're so high you can't make it." She kissed me sweetly upon the mouth. "That's what your trouble is, you're a dope fiend."

We lay there for a while, just holding on to each other. Somehow I had forgotten about how Elaine could be. I had been distracted, but I guess that's nothing unusual for me. "How do you feel? Don't feel bad," she said.

* * *

A seagull flew over us. We got dressed and went back to Lee Mellon and Elizabeth. They were looking for something and Roy Earle was there looking for something with them. It was good that I was not surprised.

"Lose something?" Elaine said.

"Yeah," Roy Earle said. "Forgot my pomegranate. I remember putting it down here somewhere. Right around here."

"It must be some place," Elizabeth said.

Lee Mellon was looking under a rock.

"I spent a dime for that pomegranate," Roy Earle said. "It means a lot to me. I bought it in Watsonville."

"We'll look over here," I said. There was nothing else to do, for after all this was the destiny of our lives. A long time ago this was our future, looking now for a lost pomegranate at Big Sur.

"What are you going to do with that pomegranate?" Lee Mellon said.

"It's going to Los Angeles with me. Big Business."

Elizabeth looked up and smiled. Lee Mellon put the rock back in place so you couldn't tell it had been moved.

A SECOND ENDING

A seagull flew over us. We got dressed and went back to Lee Mellon and Elizabeth. They were just as we had left them.

Elizabeth was sitting on a white rock and Lee Mellon

was lying flat on his back, sprawled flung out on the rough sand.

Nothing had changed. They were exactly the same.

They looked like photographs in an old album. They didn't say anything and we sat down beside them. That's where you've seen us before.

A THIRD ENDING

A seagull flew over us, its voice running with the light, its voice passing historically through songs of gentle color. We closed our eyes and the bird's shadow was in our ears.

A FOURTH ENDING

A seagull flew over us. We got dressed and went back to Lee Mellon and Elizabeth. Roy Earle was there with them. It was good that I was not surprised.

They were all standing together in the surf and throwing Roy Earle's money into the Pacific Ocean. Hundred dollar bills scattered off their hands.

"What are you doing?" I said.

Lee Mellon turned toward me, hundred dollar bills still falling off his hands, floating down onto the water.

"Roy Earle doesn't want his money any more, and we're helping him throw it in the ocean."

"We don't want it either," Elizabeth said.

"All this money ever did was bring me here," Roy Earle volunteered as the hundred dollar bills fluttered like birds onto the sea.

"You can have it," he said, addressing the waves. "Take it on home with you."

And they did.

A FIFTH ENDING

A seagull flew over us. I reached up and ran my hand along his beautiful soft white feathers, feeling the arch and rhythm of his flight. He slipped off my fingers away into the sky.

186,000 ENDINGS PER SECOND

Then there are more and more endings: the sixth, the 53rd, the 131st, the 9,435th ending, endings going faster and faster, more and more endings, faster and faster until this book is having 186,000 endings per second.